DAHLIA ROSE

DR

Royal Fire

DAHLIA ROSE

Royal Fire

Chapter One

Her feet pounded rhythmically against the wet sidewalk as she ran. Sweat rolled down the back of her t-shirt and into the top of her jeans as the oppressive heat tried to be stingy with every breath.

"If he thinks he's getting away tonight, he is sadly mistaken," Lyra muttered and kept pace.

She didn't even blink when he jumped a tall fence to go through the park at night. Lyra cleared it easily and ran, gaining on her suspect with the intent of catching him and possibly biting his head off A siren screeched as her partner followed. In actuality, he had no choice because she was out of the car when the suspect caught a whiff of the set-up with a low key dealer and booked it. There was no way she was losing him now. Tollie was responsible for three overdoses with the new strain of ecstasy he was peddling in the street. Being a chemist just meant he could tweak the recipe just a little, but this one killed people, and Lyra was determined to get him off the street.

"Get to the ground now or I swear to Odin…"

He laughed at her words as she yelled and that just pissed her off more. Tired of playing with him, she increased her pace, feeling the fire within her burn as she gained. He was her prey now. He was already down the stairs that led to where the summer symphony orchestra played their Friday night shows. Without hesitation, she launched off the first step and felt the freedom of gliding for just a minute before she landed on him and his knees gave way. They hit the hard ground together, but he broke her fall.

"I told you to stop running." Lyra put a knee in his back and grabbed his hands to cuff them.

"You ain't got nothing on me," Tollie sneered and then gasped. "How heavy are you, lady?"

"Are you calling me fat?" She dug her hand in his pockets to pull out bags of his products. "And what's this, huh? Candy, skittles?"

"You planted that," Tollie said, outraged.

"Uh-huh." She got to her feet and dragged him up to stand. "I'm sure a judge will believe that."

Her partner came running up, and he put his hands on his knees. Lyra watched with amusement as Everett tried to catch his breath and held up one hand to indicate he couldn't talk quite yet.

Finally, he straightened his lean body and glared at her. "I thought we discussed this, Lyra."

"I'm faster. We all know this, and I wasn't letting this jack-hole get away."

"First off, it's either jackass or asshole, pick one," Everett replied. "And I saw you launch like a fucking rocket off the steps. One of these days you'll break something or worse."

She patted her partner on his shoulder. "Then you'll be there to back me up."

"Or you'll kill me first," Everett muttered as he walked in front of her.

Lyra laughed and handed Everett the evidence as they walked back to their car. It was actually her car, but Everett loved the Charger SRT more than she did. She actually offered it to him one time as a birthday present, yeah… they were drunk, but she could afford it. Being a princess had its perks. Here she was, simple Lyra Temple, a good cop born into money. Everett refused and borrowed the car on occasion for dates.

He wasn't a bad looking man at all; sandy blond hair he barely kept neat and a beard that was more like a five o'clock shadow. He was six three, and to her six feet tall a good match in height. With his looks in Arizona he was a bit of heart breaker—anywhere really. Lyra recalled taking him with her to the South Beach house and all the women who were attracted to him. They were friends, but he still didn't know her secret. After four years of being partners, she was still unsure how he would react.

He'd called for backup when she ran and an SUV with two uniformed officers waited at the car. The officers got Tollie into the back of the squad car as he complained about police brutality and anything he could spew. She stood with Everett, still filled with energy and almost ready to crawl out of her own skin.

"Back to the precinct and we can write this up," Everett said. "I'll even spring for burgers at our desk."

"Can you handle it on your own?" Lyra asked hopefully. "I need to get something done, and it's important."

"You okay?" Everett asked, instantly on alert.

Lyra nodded and smiled. "I just crashed hard from the chase and a migraine is coming on. I need to visit my acupuncturist before it gets worse."

It always amazed her how easy it was to make up random lies to protect her secret. But each time she gave Everett some silly excuse, she felt bad because he was one of the truest friends she had outside of Trixie.

"You and these damn headaches." Everett cupped her cheeks and looked into her eyes as if he could see her feigned illness. "Yeah, I can see the pupils trying to keep out light already. Go ahead, get out of here and feel better."

"Take the car, my doc isn't too far away," Lyra said. "I'll see you in the morning."

"You sure?" Everett asked.

Lyra was already walking away. "By Odin, I never say anything I don't mean, Everett Craig. Goodnight."

"You and your weird sayings," he called after her with a laugh.

Lyra began to run, and she picked up speed, finally arriving at the old catholic church. She used the old metal stairs on the outside of the building to climb up to the roof. Lyra shed her clothes quickly and gave herself over to the second nature within herself. It ran like electricity along her every nerve and a sigh of pleasure escaped Lyra's lips as she gave herself over to the change. Her wings spread out and the warmth of the wind made her stretch them out wide. Rain was in the air.

She scented it easily in her second nature and turned north toward Catalina Mountains, one of her favorite spots. With a flap of her massive wings, she took to the air and lifted her nose in the wind in happiness. She lived in human form more often than not because after the Shen War, King Orin wanted the dragons to fade back to obscurity. Lyra couldn't blame him. The pictures and video clips of the last war had people so concerned even the government started an investigation.

She knew for a fact that the king and his court spent millions of dollars spinning it as an elaborate hoax. They certainly didn't need her flying around and making people start talking again. She loved taking on her second nature; being a dragon had its perks, and this was one of them. With the wind under her wings and the first drops of rain coursing down her scales, nothing could compare. Police work took a close second, because by god she loved it. The stories she heard about Paladin didn't compare. She absolutely loved the earth realm and not one thing would change that.

Lyra landed in the dry earth, trying hard to soak up the rain that was coming down harder. She spread her wings and let out a cry of delight. The answering call came across on the wind, startling her more than the crack of thunder. A swatch of lightning cut through the sky, and Lyra saw the form coming toward her from the dark sky. *Ugh, what the hell now?* She began to shift from her dragon form. Nudity meant nothing to a dragon, and Lyra waited as the other dragon landed and began to return to human form. She gritted her teeth when she saw who it was, and the cocky walk as he moved toward her only served to aggravate her all the more.

"What are you doing here?" The rain that coursed down her body didn't chill her in the least.

"Is that any way to greet your betrothed?" he asked.

"Dael, I wouldn't marry you if you were the last male in any of the realms," Lyra answered. "Again, why are you here?"

"Time to end this nonsense, Lyra, daughter of Hamon," Dael answered. "It's time to come home and marry the head of the warrior guard."

"That's not happening." Lyra put her hands on her hips. "On either point."

A slow smile spread across Dael's lips. "You have no choice in the matter, a princess must do as she is told."

"This princess lives by her own rules, and any man or dragon who touches me will learn that really quickly." Looking him up and down, Lyra smiled. "Do you dare?"

"Bruise such sweet, delectable skin, those firm nipples beg for my touch," he murmured and stepped closer.

"Oh, step off, will you?" Lyra snapped. "That may work with the women on Paladin who warm your bed, but I won't be one. You are a notorious man-whore, Dael. My father lives by the old ways but my mother gave me this life, this world. It is by the king's permission I am here. Are you defying him?"

"Maybe he changed his mind?" Dael said in defiance.

Lyra laughed. "Then by all means, let's go through the portal and ask him." She saw his eyes shift nervously. "Yeah, I thought so."

"I could force you to come with me," he said coldly. "I will have my wife and my dowry and…"

"Your title, Dael?" Lyra questioned. "Not from me. Run on home now like a good soldier."

She assessed the man in front of her. He was handsome—strikingly so—with dark hair and a jawline most men would jealous of. Like most of the warriors, he was tall with broad shoulders and lean hips. But while the women of Paladin swooned over the leader of the warrior guard, she felt nothing. His cocky attitude, as well as greed and open lust for money and power was in his eyes. That was not the Paladin way and soon it would come to a head for him. For her, she was unsure where the dice would fall.

"Anything else, Dael?" Lyra asked. "Or can I go home and have some dinner and a nice brandy?"

He suddenly grabbed her by the shoulders and brought her naked body against his. "One of these days, you will learn to submit, and I will take that pride right out of you."

"Then that's the day I would be dead." Lyra lifted her eyes defiantly. "Threatening to beat a princess of Paladin… I wonder what punishment that holds?"

He shoved her away, but Lyra never lost her balance. She watched as Dael shifted to his dragon form and strode in the opposite direction. With a flap of his massive onyx wings, he took to the sky and soon was out of sight. Her shoulders slumped with a sigh. Lyra knew what had to be done. Going home after an enjoyable night flight wouldn't be in the cards at that point. Instead, she returned to her own dragon form and took to the skies. Since the war and the fall of the Shen, the guardian Larissa was allowed to open more portals that had been closed for the protection of the earth realm. The magic within her as her dragon sensed the rifts and tears in the fabric between worlds only opened for her kind.

A journey that would take hours by car took only minutes within the folds in time, and she flew out over the tree line near the rise of a familiar old farmhouse. She landed in secret, shifting between the trees and finding a cloak in the shed that was built close by to avoid walking through the woods nude. It was past ten when she went up the familiar back steps and knocked on the door. Ginna and Kalv now spent half the time in Texas and the rest in Paladin which meant their children knew of both worlds. It was because of her uncle Kalv that her father allowed her to be a part of the human society after her mother died.

Ginna looked up from the dough she was kneading on the table when Lyra opened the door. "Hey, Sugar! What are you doing in this neck of the woods?"

"Hi Auntie G." Lyra smiled warmly. "Where's everyone?"

"Past ten, Lyra. The kids are in bed, they have school in the morning," Ginna said with amusement. "That was you around seven years ago."

"And I was twenty now learning this realm," Lyra pointed out. "You did the right thing by letting Sari and Ben learn both from early on. Where is Uncle Kalv? I need some advice from both of you."

"Ooh, cop stuff. Is there a murder? Are you on a hot case?" Ginna asked excitedly. "He's out in the barn, fixing the pen for the cows ready to birth…"

The door creaked as it opened, and her uncle stepped inside. "I heard you in the woods, like a damn bull in a china shop. I finished up what I was doing and came in."

"And here he is." Ginna waved her hand in a flourish.

"You're silly." He grinned and kissed her on the cheek as he went to the sink. "How is the policing of the fair Arizona going, Lyra?"

"Caught a guy pushing a new type of ecstasy today," Lyra said proudly. "He thought he could outrun me."

"And you proved him wrong." Kalv ruffled her hair. "It's not raining and your hair is soaked."

"It was in the mountains outside Tulsa. I went for a night flight; that's what I wanted to talk to you about," Lyra explained. "Dael followed me and we had a kind of confrontation."

Kalv's mouth set into a grim line. "Do I need to go collect a body and explain to Orin?"

Lyra grinned, loving his faith in her abilities. "He's okay, but he demanded I come home and marry his whoring ass as he grabbed me. He vowed to make me submit, and I'm not that type. Uncle, he's greedy. He wants power, and he thinks that marrying me will get it. Dael's openly blunt about this fact, and that's not what Paladin is about. After the war and the removal of the corrupt caretaker sect, Orin's rule followed his father's. No greed amongst us, yet he's not happy just being the leader of the warrior guard. He wants to be royalty."

Orin poured her a cup of coffee and one for himself before sitting across from her. Ginna then placed a big bowl of pasta and bread in front of her as well and Lyra smiled. This was how they always were, working in unison without even a word, kind of how she and Everett worked as partners.

"He grabbed you, and that is a no-no. Your body is yours and trying to make you submit..." Ginna made an angry sound. "I want to kick him in the balls."

"Is my father behind this?" Lyra asked. "He wasn't pleased that I chose earth realm instead of Paladin."

"Hamon would know better," Kalv muttered. "At least I hope he would. Orin already said he would not honor any betrothed couples unless the female was in consent. One look at your face and Orin would know Dael was on some bullshit."

Lyra grinned. "He would be on that stuff for sure because I can't stand that warrior. But what should I do?"

Ginna sat down. "I tell you what we should do. I go upstairs and get that Louisville slugger I keep behind the door, and we go to Paladin and—"

Kalv cut off her angry words by covering her hand. "What you do is go to my office and write a formal letter on that royal letterhead you keep here. Then I will deliver it to Orin and the Paladin court myself. Orin will call Hamon and Dael before him and end this nonsense immediately."

"Will I need to be there?" Lyra asked worriedly. "I try to avoid conflict with my father when I go home to recharge. He's still not happy with my choices."

"He's just gonna have to get over it," Ginna said firmly. "You've been gone for years now, and you go home when you can. Forcing a marriage doesn't help you or him be closer."

"He thinks the world corrupted mama," Lyra said sadly. "She belonged to this world, and yet he hates it."

"Your father expected your mother to be everything she wasn't, and that was what forced that catalyst." Kalv sighed and pulled his hair back before using the tie he kept around his hand to create a ponytail. "Now he wants the same from you. My brother should see he is repeating his past mistakes."

"I'll go write that letter, and then I have to

head back home. I'm on an eight, and we have a sting set up if we can get my perp to crack."

"No. First you eat, then you write," Ginna said firmly. "Then you crash on the sofa and eat ice cream and watch TV or nap for a little. I bet you've been up all dang day."

"Yes, Auntie Ginna," Lyra said dutifully but she smiled at the warmth that filled her. Ginna was the only motherly caring Lyra had known for a long time.

"Good." Ginna smiled widely and clapped her hands. "Plus, you said perp, and I want to girl talk and hear all about your partner and the job from a dragon point of view. It will be good for the archives."

"Sure, it will," Kalv's voice said with humor in his voice. "Lyra, do not let her convince you to give her a ride along."

"I'll try, but she is pretty convincing," Lyra teased.

She loved the warmth of the old farmhouse where she learned about this new world before her first tentative steps within it. Lyra knew that her uncle and aunt would help her find the right answers. Hopefully, adding the formality of it would get Dael off her back. He wanted to bite her neck and hold her in submission, and she would crack his skull if he even dared. Petitioning the king and the Paladin court was the best answer. Dael could write her off as the one who didn't want him and ran away.

Chapter Two

Being able to sleep in was one of the luxuries that Lyra favored. She got back to Tucson around two a.m. and showered before slipping between the Egyptian cotton sheets and thick, weighted blankets. She kept her central air on cool so that her house was cold, and she was snuggled on the soft mattress with five plus pounds of covers on top of her.

"Lyra, wake up, we have a case," Everett's voice entered her dreams trying to force her into reality.

"Get out of my dreams, Ev. I'm sunning naked in the lilac grass of Paladin," she murmured and moved further down in the blankets.

"You're where now? What?" She felt hands moving over the covers. "Where the hell are you under all this crap? How are you not smothered to death?"

Lyra sat up with a sigh. "You're real, aren't you, and I'm not dreaming."

"Unfortunately, no. I was on my way here to pick you up and got the call. Homicide with possible kidnapping," Everett explained. "Let's get a move on, I got coffee waiting."

"The good kind?" Lyra slipped naked from the bed and walked toward the bathroom.

"Jesus, Lyra warn someone will ya?" Everett choked out and looked away quickly.

"That's what you get for breaking into my place, flagrant nudity," she called with a laugh. She went into the walk-in closet to find clothes. "What's with you people and the naked body, anyway?"

"Were you raised in a nudist colony or something? Did they give you some peyote because you talk about lilac grass a lot," he called back. "And I have a key, the one you gave me."

"Fine, fine, I'll be out in five," she answered.

After brushing her teeth and trying to give some semblance of order to her hair, Lyra pulled out the comfortable chocolate brown slacks that hugged her hips and paired it with a white t-shirt that molded against her curves. With a light blazer to match and her trusty black boots, she was ready to go and walked out of her dressing room.

"I'm strange, remember. It was the first thing you said to me when we partnered up." She sat on the bed and bent over to tie her boots.

"You talked like a medieval storyteller

sometimes," he pointed it. "It's getting better, but hey, I like ya."

"I feel so much better with your approval," Lyra said dryly. "Are you driving or am I?"

Everett tossed the key at her. "I drove here, try not to kill me. I'd like to get to the scene in one piece."

"Hey, I'm a good driver," she protested as they left her bedroom and went through the living room. She pressed the button to open the automatic blinds that revealed the sun and the pool outside.

"I swear, if I didn't know you were rich, I'd say you were on the take to live like this," Everett said.

"I already had to hear about being a rich princess playing cop so I can take only so much before I kick someone's ass," Lyra said and gave him a look. "Even yours."

He slapped her on the shoulder. "I know better than to fuck with you, and even though I gave you heat, I could tell you were a damn fine cop, good instincts. I swear you can smell drugs on a perp or tell where they're hiding."

If he only knew, she thought. The sunlight was warm against her face when they stepped outside. Lyra lifted her head, loving the feel of rays on her skin, and inside her, her dragon purred, begging to lie out in the sun. Promising a day to relax next to the pool seemed to appease her second nature, and they walked to the car.

"Wanna show up at the crime scene in my new Bugatti?" she asked wickedly.

"You got a new…" Everett shook his head. "No, do not tempt me, woman. I get enough flack about sucking on your rich tits."

She slid behind the wheel of the car, and he got in and slammed the door. "They actually give you shit about me?"

"You are seriously naïve. There's a bet on if we're fucking or not and how long it will take for brass to put us with different partners because of it," he said.

"That's utterly ridiculous." She maneuvered out of her driveway and after he gave her the address, she headed out of the exclusive neighborhood gates. "I haven't ever mated with anyone so to think I'm boinking my way through the Tucson Police Department is silly and so stereotypical."

Everett choked on his coffee. "You mean, you haven't slept with another cop, right? I'm assuming that's what you mean by mated."

Lyra took a sip of her coffee and found it still warm and delicious. "No, I mean I never mated, or as you say, slept with anyone, ever."

Everett looked at her in shock. "But you're twenty-seven."

Lyra shrugged. "So? It's in my nature that if I give myself to someone it's going to be forever."

"That's a very innocent thought process. Not everything works out," Everett laughed.

"In my culture, we mate for life." Lyra kept her eyes on the road and her words were matter-of-fact. There was no other way to explain her kind and how they loved.

Everett laughed and waved his finger at her. "I knew you were in a cult."

Lyra ignored the comment. "Should I tell everyone I'm a virgin, so they get off your back?"

"Christ no! That will earn you a whole new set of problems," Everett answered quickly. "You'd be fending off cops trying to take advantage of you left and right."

She shook her head. "It's all very confusing. First, they'd think I'm up for grabs then they'd try to get me into bed because I'm a virgin. What in the hell is wrong with the male species?"

"We are a horny bunch who thinks with our dicks," Everett answered honestly. "I think it's sweet that you are waiting for Mr. Right. It's like you're a throwback from a different era, and it's refreshing. Even though that cult has you a bit too free with information and nudity."

Lyra smiled and let that comment go as she weaved through morning traffic and yelled at stupid drivers in her way. She always wondered why humans seemed to be so fixated on nudity, but still the pornography industry was booming, and it was so easily accessible on the internet. She could only assume they liked to keep their vices hidden, and that was one of the reasons she liked being on the force. She could smell a lie as easily as if it was a flower in bloom. The police cars when she pulled in front of the apartment complex made her heart race just a bit faster. There was nothing like this on Paladin, nothing that gave her such an adrenaline rush. They stepped out of the car and walked toward the police tape. A patrolman held it up so they could go under it.

"Carlos, do we have a baby yet?" Lyra asked the man in uniform.

He smiled broadly. "Not yet, and Joanie is completely miserable. She wants him out, says he is sitting on her bladder and she can hardly walk."

"Did you do what I told you with the baseball and her back?" Lyra asked. "Did she like the baby shower gift?"

"I do and that really helps her rest at night," he answered enthusiastically. "Like the gift, are you crazy? She loves it—a circle crib with matching bedding. She broke down crying when she saw it and said it's too much."

"You tell her nothing but the best for that baby, and I get dibs on baby snuggles." She patted his shoulder with a smile. "Body back there?"

"Yep, go through the walkway to the pool," Carlos said. "You can snuggle or babysit whenever you like."

She went through with a wave, put on the requisite booties, and followed the crime scene techs to the body.

"You bought them a round crib? Isn't that a bit extravagant?" Everett asked.

"Why should it be an issue?" A hand hung off the patio chair.

"Because most everyone else gave them baby clothes, diapers, milk, and baby bags from the registry," Everett pointed out. "Giving them such a luxury gift makes the rest of us look cheap."

"So, you're saying hide my money and pretend I don't have shit to make everyone feel better," Lyra snapped. "It seems there are extra rules for me to fit in and make people comfortable. But anyone else can do what they want and still critique me and wonder who I'm fucking."

"Lower your voice please." Everett's voice was low and calm.

She threw up her hands. "Why everyone thinks I'm a rich, stuck-up bitch sleeping with you. Hey Louie, how much do you have bet on me being naked with Ev here?"

"Twenty-five," the older man said walking by. "I, for a fact, do not think you are a rich, stuck-up bitch. Buy me a car if you want."

"I just might do that," Lyra called after him, and he gave her a thumbs-up sign. It seemed people's perceptions of her at work bothered Lyra more than she realized, and that was annoying to her.

"You went from happy and hey everything's cool to biting my head off," Everett pointed out.

"You went from my partner having my back to trying to make me pretend to be something I'm not," Lyra shot back. "Like everyone else in this realm, you have the choice to like me or not. Partner with me or not but don't ever expect me to act or be less to make you or anyone else comfortable."

"Realm?" Everett's lips twitched.

"Suck on a mint," she said sweetly.

"That is not an insult," he said walking around the body.

She followed suit, assessing the body before working outwards to the actual scene for evidence. This was a young woman, no older than thirty and in seemingly good health. Lyra inhaled and smelled a strong odor but not like any drug whose scent would coincide with an overdose. There was no bruising or strangulation mark, no defense wounds; it looked like she just sat in the sun and fell asleep to die.

"How do they figure kidnapping?" Lyra asked.

One of the crime scene techs dusting came over. "They found toys, coloring books, and water wings for a child but no kid is around. They started a search and no sign of a kid wandering in the area."

"If she had a child and he or she thought mama was sleeping would they go exploring?" Lyra asked. "Was the building searched to see if a kid is looking for home base?"

"We found her key card, she is in apartment twelve B. No sign of a kid, no sign of a struggle," the tech answered.

"Married." Everett pointed at her finger. "We need to get the husband to come in."

"We have a car heading to his office. He's a dentist." Louie came back over. "There's something over in the bushes by the towel rack that you might want to see."

"Okay," Lyra murmured and squatted down to look at the body more closely.

"Anything seem off? Your instincts are usually on point," Everett asked.

She shook her head. "This one is unusual, to say the least. Look at her eyes, the color is off somehow."

"Could it be the post-mortem clouding?" Everett asked.

"No, this isn't milky…" She stood up and stretched. "Let's see what Louie found."

They walked over to where an evidence marker was and what was at the base of the bushes made her heart shudder and almost freeze in her chest. The rich vibrant red of the color was all too familiar, the weaving pattern unique to… Paladin. *The caretakers, Paladin… what the hell!* Her breath quickened as she looked down at the cloth and then took in her surroundings and the people who stood outside the police line, watching, observing. Which one of them knew her secret? Was this a message for her or were the caretakers up to no good? The whole sect was disbanded after the great war and they went back to their lives. All knew some were still in search of power even if they kept it hidden well. Was this the first step in a new terror against the earth realm?

"Lyra!" Everett calling her name dragged her from her dark thoughts.

"I'm listening," she lied.

"Yeah, no you weren't," Everett answered. "Do you know this scarf?"

She shook her head and added another lie to the cache she was hoarding. "No. I was so startled — the color, for one. Who would wear this for a kidnapping and murder?"

"Maybe it didn't start out that way?" Everett said. "I'd bet my mother's good silver that this is a love triangle. Mistress couldn't get what she wanted, decided to confront the wife, and it went bad and she took the kid."

"Why take the child and stop wagering your mother's possessions," Lyra said.

"It's a saying… never mind." He shook his head. "The mistress could think taking the kid would give her some leverage against the father or police."

"All it will give her is an extra felony," Lyra said. She doubted very much that Everett's assessment was correct. The red color of the sash caught her attention again. No, it was much, much worse if her world and this realm were to collide again.

"Log everything into evidence and let's get the body onto Frederick's slab and see what he can tell us. I want pictures of everything before it's moved," Everett said to the techs working around them then made a flourished move in Lyra's direction. "M'lady, would you like an escort to the upstairs apartment where we can dissect our victim's life?"

"And you call me weird." Lyra moved around him and after a final glance at the body, made her way to the elevators and the fifth floor with her partner. "We should canvas the neighbors before we even talk to the husband, see what they say as opposed to what he tells us."

"Not so happy life, the neighbors are the first to know," Everett affirmed. "You go left and I'll go right."

With a quick nod, she walked to the end of the hall to work her way back to the victim's home. One apartment was vacant, and the other tenant was at work. On her third try, she found a young mother who answered the door holding a baby bottle under her chin and feeding a baby. Her chocolate brown hair was a messy bun, and she was still wearing a bathrobe. Looking at her disheveled appearance, Lyra had no doubt she hadn't seen regular clothes in a while from taking care of the baby.

"Can I help you?" She took the bottle and held it so she could look up at Lyra.

Lyra showed her the badge clipped at her waist. "Detective Lyra Temple, Tucson PD. Do you know the resident of twelve B?"

"Monica?" The young mother frowned. "Yes, we're friends. Why?"

"What's her last name?" Lyra asked, taking out her phone to make notes.

"Monica Hart, her husband is Geoff," she replied to Lyra. "You're scaring me, what happened to Monica?"

"I'm sorry to tell you but she was found deceased, downstairs by the pool," Lyra said gently, and she moved quickly when the woman's knees almost buckled. "Okay, come on now, let's get you sitting down with the tiny human."

The mother giggled. "Tiny human, that's funny. You said Monica was dead?"

"What's your name, ma'am?" Lyra needed her to focus and get past the shock if any pertinent information was to be gleaned from her friendship with the victim.

"Amy Parsons," she said weakly and looked down at the baby in her arms. "This is Vicki, she is two months old… Oh god, where's Bryce?"

"Who's Bryce?" Lyra asked.

"Monica and Geoff's son. He's two." Amy's voice rose in panic, causing the baby in her arms to fuss. "Someone has to get Geoff at work, he needs to come home to his son."

"Amy, Bryce is missing." Lyra broke the news as gently as she could and watched the woman's eyes fill with tears. "I need your help; I need to know everything you do about Monica and her son."

"She wouldn't have let him be taken, she would have fought," Amy said fiercely and held her own daughter tighter. "She worked from home so she could be a full-time mom."

"What did she do for a living?" Lyra watched how a mother's love made her want to protect her child even from the unknown. It made her wonder if her own mother had felt that way. She could barely remember the woman who died when she was a young child.

"Monica was an electrical engineer and drew the plans from home," Amy explained. "She went to the work sites if there were issues and when it was the stage to put in the wiring. I'd watch Bryce if she had to go in."

She sensed no lies or mistruth coming from Amy, but Lyra had to ask the usual questions. "How long have you known her?"

"Three years, since before she had the baby," Amy answered. "Her and my husband Jay play golf together, and we are all pretty close."

"So, no problems in their marriage, no arguments or issues?" Lyra hinted.

Amy shook her head. "No, not all! They are so in love, and we make fun of them for being so cutesy. I don't know why someone would kill her and take Bryce! I need to call my husband, I can't…"

"Go ahead and call your husband and we will get an Amber alert out on Bryce." Lyra's mind was working fast, trying to find a connection between caretakers and killing a mom or kidnapping a two-year-old. "Can I reach out to you if I have any more questions?"

"Of course, and please, if you find Bryce bring him here," Amy begged. "Until Geoff gets home, we can watch him. I was supposed to go down to the pool too, but Vicki is fussing and I'm exhausted." She gave a soft laugh and looked down at herself. "Look at me. I should shower at some point when she finally naps."

"It's okay, being a mother is one of the hardest jobs out there." Lyra gave her an encouraging smile.

"Please find who did this, find Bryce." Amy's eyes filled with tears again.

Lyra gave her a swift nod, not wanting to break her heart anymore to the fact that the baby boy was probably long gone from the area. She left, and Amy locked the deadbolt behind her before Lyra made her way back to Everett.

"Anything?" Lyra asked.

"The usual, shock, quiet family, no problems, no big fights," Evert said. "You?"

"I met her best friend Amy. The son's name is Bryce, and he's two years old," Lyra said. "Amy said they were the perfect couple, almost sickeningly adorable. To me that says hidden secrets."

Everett chuckled as they stepped into the family's apartment. "I'm sure she didn't use those words."

"I ad-libbed a little."

"Maybe they were completely and utterly in love," Everett said. "What do you have against mushy type couples?"

"Nothing at all." Lyra looked around the relatively neat apartment sans the usual toys and chaos of a two-year-old. "My aunt and uncle are very in love, but they will be the first to tell you it wasn't all peaches and cream, and there are hard times. Any couple who tries so hard to be perfect in front of everyone is hiding something in private."

"So jaded," Everett teased.

"Not all, just realistic." Lyra picked up a book and flipped through the pages. "Like my Aunt Ginna said, if you can love someone after they destroyed your barn then that's love."

"That's some country theology right there." Everett added a southern twang to his voice.

She smiled and glanced at him. "Not really.

My uncle Kalv has destroyed her barn about four times so far. But he always rebuilds it."

He shook his head. "Your family dynamic is totally unusual."

"Want to talk about your mother?" Lyra asked.

Everett shuddered. "God no, and let's not invoke the name of that woman. She shows up like a monster from a horror movie. I swear even the devil is terrified of her."

Lyra chuckled, and they processed the apartment, taking a small, framed photo of Bryce so they could have the father's approval to use it on the news. An Amber alert would be issued but with his light blond curly hair it would be easy to cut and change the color. She didn't think he was in danger; if that had been the case, they'd have a tiny body along with his mother's. That would have pissed her off to no end because hurting children would possibly cause her to char the killer to ash. Someone wanted that child, and Monica was in the way. Now it was up to them to figure out why and how she was killed.

Chapter Three

Later that night, she mulled over the royal red sash of the Caretakers at the crime scene. She sat at the bar while she watched her friend close for the night. Trixie was the only other person besides her family in Texas to know about her true form. It happened at a time when loneliness assaulted her senses. Being a rookie and so new to living was taking a toll on her, and her secret slipped to the one person she could talk to: Trixie.

Her friend never revealed her confidence, and Lyra even took her to Paladin once with the King's permission. At this point, the cocktail that Trixie made wasn't bringing her the same joy in taste. Instead, she stared into the pink liquid as if searching for answers.

"You're supposed to drink that." Trixie came back behind the bar. Her curly, short hair had the front dyed hot pink. She was mixed race just like Lyra except there wasn't a dragon living within her body as well. "It's my new creation. I call it a pink lemonade fizz."

"I like the taste," Lyra answered. "I taste sours, vermouth, gin, pink lemonade, and simple syrup."

"I hate that sense of smell and taste you have."

"Hey, I could tell that guy was lying to you about not being married, so don't knock the dragon senses." Lyra took another sip of her drink.

Trixie raised her shot glass. "Touché. The fact you could smell a hint of his wife's perfume saved me misery upon misery. Now what got you in that dragon head of yours?"

Lyra explained what they found at the crime scene, knowing that whatever she told her friend would be kept in confidence. Expressing her fear and anxiety about the caretakers and the thought of them trying to prey on humans again made the situation all too real.

Trixie leaned her elbows on the bar. "So, did you get a scent off the sash?"

Lyra shook her head. "Nothing, not even detergent or a scent of home."

"Could it have been planted to throw a curve ball at you?" Trixie asked.

"No one knows about my second nature, and I would sense another like me in the vicinity." Lyra sighed.

"Your asshole fiancée could be trying to fuck

with your life." Trixie went back to her task of turning off lights behind the glass of the wall full of alcohol bottles.

"I'd have scented him straight off and possibly shot him." Lyra stood and began putting stools on the top of tables. "Still, it's a possibility I have to look into. He could have a human helping him try to disrupt my life. It makes no sense telling my uncle or the Paladin court until I have something more definite."

"You gonna tell Everett?" Trixie prodded.

Lyra looked at her and shrugged helplessly. "What exactly? Hey Ev, guess what? I'm a dragon shifter, and there was a huge war no human ever heard of, but these caretakers decided to work with the bad guys. Oh, and I found one of their sashes at our crime scene."

Trixie threw a wash rag at her. "Yeah, something like that. You've been partners for over four years, and I think you can trust him."

"Maybe," Lyra murmured. The thought terrified her. "I've had to lie to him so much… And he is big on honesty, especially after how much his mother screwed him up."

"All the more reason to tell him now," Trixie explained. "Trust me, if these caretakers are involved there is no way you can hide it if it affects the case."

"Hawke would make the whole thing go away, but Everett would sniff out a cover up so damn quick…" Lyra made a frustrated sound. "Bless it, nothing can ever be easy, could it?"

"That's this life and living thing we're doing." Trixie smiled gently. "Hey, if he doesn't believe you, you can always play if off and tell him he's crazy or was hallucinating."

Lyra threw the wash rag back at her friend. "Ha-ha, very funny."

"So, I'm coming home with you tonight. I want to use your pool and sauna," Trixie announced.

"You only like me for me stuff," Lyra teased. "If you're swimming, I am too. We can mix margaritas and order pizza…"

The conversation was halted abruptly when a loud sound of splintering wood and shattered glass cut them off. Trixie screamed while Lyra went instantly on the defensive when two men came in with weapons.

"We ain't here to hurt no one, we just want the cash," the first gunman said.

"Maybe a little something else," the second one gave a little giggle. "Two pretty women…"

He didn't get a chance to finish. With or without a gun, Lyra wasn't letting it go down like that. The closest thing to her hand was a chair that she had put on a lower table only a moment before. With quick reflexes, she threw it in the direction of the men with such force it made the first assailant scream when it his arm. The gun fired before he dropped it, and Lyra caught sight of Trixie ducking behind the bar. His friend swung around, firing his gun in her direction and Lyra felt the bullet hit her shoulder.

She grunted in pain, and the dragon within her screamed in rage. She caught the injured man's hand and deftly swung it high behind his back, making him cry out in pain. She then shoved him toward his partner. They hit, together and fumbled a bit. The first attacker came at her again, she met him with a high kick to the side of the head. The other man swung, and she caught his arm and tugged. It brought his shoulder down close to the ground. She punched him so hard he crumpled to the floor. It all seemed to go by in a flash, but in the end, Trixie was safe.

"Holy fuck." Trixie rushed out from behind the bar. "Lyra, you got shot!"

She blew out a breath. "I'll be okay. I can feel my body expelling the metal already. I have to change my shirt and hide the wound before the police gets here. Call it in; give them my badge number tell them a cop is on scene."

"Don't you need a hospital?" Trixie asked with worry in her voice.

She shook her head. "I'll be fine. We heal quick. It nicked the bone and that will take a little while longer to heal. Call it in."

"I've got an extra shirt and a medical kit in the office." Trixie glanced at the men. "Am I safe with them?"

Lyra gave her a wicked smile. "Trust me, they're not moving."

She moved toward the back and took her shirt off just as the bullet slipped from her shoulder. She looked at the wound and pressed it with a small wince, knowing that the muscle was healing already. In order to prevent seepage, she cleaned the wound with peroxide and taped a small bandage over her shoulder. Lyra put on Trixie's t-shirt and then a zip-up sweatshirt that was thrown over the office chair. By the time she walked back to into the bar area, she heard the sirens and Trixie had taken both guns, putting them on the table away from the robbers in case they came to.

"You didn't touch these with your bare hand, did you?" Lyra asked.

Trixie rolled her eyes. "Give me some credit."

"I never got shot. They are crazy if they say I was," Lyra said.

"Mum's the word." Trixie made a locking motion at her mouth.

The police rushed in with guns drawn but Lyra showed them her badge and the man was already on the ground. The next step was to take her and Trixie's statements.

"They may need medics, guys. I think one broke his arm when he went down," Lyra said to the patrolman she knew. "Jess, the guns are over here on the table. You will find their prints all over it."

"Only you, Temple, would take down two armed men in a bar," she said dryly. "You sure you're okay?"

Lyra nodded. "Just peachy… and pissed off they thought this was the bar to break into."

"These two have been watching the movements of restaurants and bars around here. Not their first robbery in this area," Jess explained. "They probably thought tonight was a good night to hit."

"Then they were wrong," Lyra said grimly. "Bumbling idiots took themselves out more than me."

Patrolwoman Jess gave her an I-don't-believe-you look. "Uh-huh."

She watched as Trixie gave her statement and the medics came in to take the men out on the stretchers. Five minutes later, while she was wondering how they would secure Trixie's door, Everett rushed in.

"I heard the call on the radio—officer involved robbery." Everett cupped her cheeks and moved her head from side to side as if inspecting her for bruises. "Soon as they said this address, I knew it was you and Trixie. Are you both okay?"

"We're fine. Those guys weren't too great at robberies." Lyra gave him a reassuring smile.

"One said you broke his arm and the other guy is screaming he shot you." Everett gave her a dark look.

She turned around. "As you can see, no bullet holes on me. When they collided with each other he may have thought he fired the gun, but he didn't."

"How did they collide?" Everett asked.

"I distracted the first guy and shoved him at this friend, then they went down. I think that's when he broke his arm," Lyra lied smoothly.

Everett blew out a breath. "This could have ended so much worse. Best to give them the money and let them go on their merry way."

Lyra met his gaze. "They wanted more than money, two women, alone in a bar with two gunmen, guess what else they wanted, Ev?"

"I should go shoot them myself," he said angrily.

"Is this wrapping up soon?" Trixie walked up and asked. "After this we definitely need that swim, pizza, and margaritas."

"Should be done soon. We're going to need some plywood for the door to secure this place until you can get your insurance people out here," Everett replied.

"We'll get it all together and then we can head to my place." Lyra put her arm around Trixie's shoulder with a gentle squeeze.

"I heard pizza and 'ritas," Everett's voice held curiosity.

"We'll be swimming nude, so no boys allowed." Lyra poked him in the chest.

"Hey, you don't care about nudity. You walked in the bathroom naked this morning," Everett pointed out.

"Excuse me?" Trixie looked from Lyra to Everett.

"He woke me up for work," Lyra said dryly.

"Y'all are spoilsports. I'm going to go fix your door." Everett walked away.

"So, are you always nude around your partner?" Trixie teased.

Lyra shrugged, and the soreness still in her shoulder reminded her that she had been shot. "He's like a big goof gum brother, he doesn't care and neither do I."

"The word is goofball, and yeah, I know, Paladin—y'all walk around with wangs wagging everywhere." Trixie patted her on the back. "Going to have to burst your bubble here, sweet cheeks. The way he ran in and made a beeline for you just now… he doesn't feel like you are a sibling. Tell him the truth."

Lyra thought about what Trixie said as she helped Everett with the door. After wrapping it up with the police, they were allowed to leave. Even as they swam and joked, ate pizza and drank one too many mango margaritas, she had him in the back of her mind. Her friend was right, Everett had to know about her truth, and she prayed to god she didn't lose her partner because of it.

After the night they had, Trixie crashed at her house. She left her friend sleeping in her guest bedroom and went to work the next day. Trixie's day usually started in the late afternoon anyway, and since the bar would need to be fixed, Lyra doubted she would be doing anything more than yelling at her insurance guy and meeting him to see the damage. Coming home to find her friend lounging around her pool was a definite possibility and one that Lyra didn't mind. Her father thought that the earth realm would have her running back home, begging to be married off and living in royal bliss, but Trixie and the people she helped gave her a solid connection to her mother's home, one she didn't want to give up.

While she had made a firm decision to tell Everett about her life, Lyra didn't know how to broach the subject. Most of her time had been spent hiding her second nature. How would a human male feel about her being the stronger one? Would it affect his masculinity, would he tell, or worse, want a new partner? It all made her gut clench painfully even as she took a sip of the hot gourmet coffee in her travel mug.

She would have to just tell him or show him. Right now, her focus was on the three-story building in front of her as she pulled into the parking lot. The coroner's office looked like a regular business on the outside except instead of cubicles there were rows of metal tables and body freezers lined the walls. Their business was speaking for the dead, and right now they needed to know what Monica's body had to say. Everett stood outside the door, munching on some kind of pastry and looking off into the distance like something was on his mind. He raised his hand in greeting as she parked. Lyra got out of the car, locked it, and headed his way.

"Morning, mortal," Lyra said teasingly. "What are you eating?"

"Cherry cream cheese Danish." His tone was more subdued. "I snagged one from the bullpen before I headed here. I walked, so that's my exercise for the day, and I deserved a treat."

"The precinct is just around the corner so not much of an exercise routine." She laughed, and he barely smiled. "You okay, Ev?"

"Sucky night's sleep, that's all. Let's go see what Doc Frederick has to say."

"Anything on the Amber alert?" she asked as she opened the glass door and went inside.

"Nothing at all, and we finally got the father coming in when we leave here," Everett said. "Something is absolutely off that his wife gets murdered, his kid is missing, and it takes this long for us to get a statement out of this character."

"What was his excuse to not come in again?" Lyra listened to the rhythmic sound of their footfalls heading down the hallway.

"He's an oral surgeon to the stars, and he was on a private jet heading to some spa New Mexico," Everett answered. "If I heard my wife was dead and my kid was missing, I would be fuck all of you and your teeth."

"That's because you're normal. Either way,

I'll know if he's lying when we talk to him," Lyra said firmly.

"Yeah, you and your built-in lie detector," he muttered.

"Okay, what's with you? This sixth sense works all around not just with criminals," Lyra demanded.

He avoided her question. "Let's see what Doc has."

Doc Frederick was a tall, rail thin man with tight, curled blond hair that seemed thick for his head or his frame. His one step would make two of hers, and he moved with a natural slowness that made her think of a praying mantis. The long white lab coat swung behind him as he moved. He looked up and smiled when they came in, a mouth that seemed too big for his face and made him look even more unusual, but there was no better or nicer man than Doc Frederic who cared about the dead more than most.

"Hello, Everett. You pale in the company of the lovely Detective Temple," Doc said.

"Don't pick on him, Doc, he's in a mood." Lyra smiled up at the coroner. "Do you have anything on our victim?"

Doc looked from Everett to Lyra and shrugged before walking over to one of the freezers and pulling out a slab. He pulled back the white sheet to reveal the body of Monica Hart, clean and devoid of color except for the garish Y incision that now marred perfect skin. For a moment, Lyra wondered what would happen to her body when she died being part human? Paladin dragons turned to shimmering dust when their souls went back to the gods who created them. Their souls went on to their forefathers to feast at their tables of the glorious dead, the ones who fought and died as warriors. But she was half human. Would she be like her father or mother's people? The thought of lying out on a cold metal surface if she died made her feel ill.

"Monica Hart, thirty, no signs of trauma to her body but she is dead as a doornail," Doc said.

"Yep, we can see that. How did she die?" Everett asked.

"Nicotine poisoning. High levels in her urine and blood, the symptoms had to be terrible as she died. Someone injected it between her toes," Doc said.

"Her eyes were this weird color, why?" Lyra asked.

"Not many people wouldn't have caught that," Doc said, pleased. "This is why I like you, Lyra. You are magnificent at assessment. Leave the doldrums of being in the force and come work with me."

"I like my job, but I'll keep that in mind." Lyra smiled.

He covered his heart. "I shall have to tarry forth. The odd color came from a new eye surgery where a hard contact is inserted behind the cornea. It is used to give people with certain eye conditions better vision. She used it cosmetically."

"Why are women so worried about looks?" Everett sighed.

Lyra snorted. "This from a man who dates women who look like they came out of magazines."

"Hey, I've dated women who were a solid five out of ten, and they were great," Everett said in defense.

Lyra rolled her eyes. "How magnanimous of you to give them your time to make them feel worthy."

"Stop shoving that foot deeper in your mouth," Doc advised her partner. "In any case, she was a perfectly beautiful woman without the breast augmentation and liposuction, tummy tuck…"

"She had a kid so maybe the tummy tuck was to fix that," Everett said.

Doc frowned. "What are you talking about? She never had a child."

"Doc, we have an amber alert out for a two-year-old boy who is her child. Her best friend confirms it and pictures are all over that apartment of her holding a baby," Lyra said.

"I can tell you with all certainty, she never had a baby," Doc said firmly. "Maybe a surrogate was used. It's the rage now to have someone else carry your child."

"Guess that's another question we have to ask Mr. Hart." Everett looked down at the body. "Thanks Doc. Let us know if anything else comes up."

"I hope you find the child." Doc's voice held sadness. Lyra knew that children cases affected him the worst. "Bye, my darling Lyra."

She stood on her tiptoe to kiss the man who dwarfed her six-foot height. "Bye, Doc, and I have those cherries coming in for you."

"Bless you." Doc blew her a kiss as they left.

"Want a ride back?" Lyra asked Everett as they walked out the building.

"Nah, I'll walk," he said stiffly.

Enough was enough. She grabbed his forearms. "Since when is my car a bad thing? You borrow it all the time. Are they teasing you again?"

"None of that," Everett answered and turned away.

"Then what?" Lyra heard the pleading tone in

her voice. "What's wrong with you that you are treating me like an unwanted stepchild?"

He whirled on her as they stood on the sidewalk. "I don't like lies, and my partner feeding me bullshit usually puts me in a bad mood."

Her heart picked up in speed. "What lies did I tell?"

He moved until they were nose-to-nose. "That gun last night was fired. I could smell it when they logged it into evidence. I went back and found blood on the ground. You and Trixie didn't clean it up all the way. Sloppy work, detective."

"Ev…" She didn't know what to say

He grabbed her shoulders suddenly and squeezed. Although the wound was healed on the outside, the inside was still mending. Lyra winced.

"Yeah, I thought so," he said angrily.

"Everett, we have a lot to talk about but please let me explain. I wanted to tell you for so long…"

"Yeah, we do, but right now we have a job and a suspect waiting for us. I'll see you back at the precinct."

He turned on his heel and strode away angrily. Lyra watched him go, and in her heart she was terrified. Her time was up, and the truth would have to be told. How it would end? She was unsure, but Lyra got into her car to make the short drive to the police department. He was right, they had a job to do.

She was already in the detective bullpen when he walked in. He flicked a glance at her before directing her with his head toward the interview room. She noted that others, people they worked with, picked up on the tension and passed knowing glances between each other. *Their betting pool is probably going up,* Lyra thought as she followed him. His attitude irritated her because he had no clue what was going on. The secrets were to protect him and herself. Lyra shook her head, knowing she was wrong to hide the truth, so she was willing to take the cold shoulder up to a point.

Interview room three held drab gray walls and a simple office table that was against a far wall and bolted into the floor. It was the same with the chair that Mr. Geoff Hart sat in. After a few incidents where suspects threw chairs, department heads thought it was best to minimize projectiles in the rooms. People always saw lieutenants watching interviews through one-way glass mirrors while they tried to glean information.

She had never seen a room set up that way. Instead, there were two cameras mounted on the wall with sound capabilities. They were recorded at all times to keep both parties safe and to have a recording she and Everett could go back through. If stories changed, there it was held in time, exactly what was said. Lyra could smell Geoff's Hart's sweat and the stink of deceit on him. He would not be an easy person to talk to.

"I'm Detective Everett Craig, my partner, Detective Temple," Everett said as he sat down. Lyra chose to stand.

"What happened to my wife, my son?" Geoff Hart demanded. "Shouldn't you be out looking for him?"

"Shouldn't you have been here from the time we reached you through your nurse?" Everett responded.

Geoff made a disgusted sound in his throat. "I was already on a plane. It's not like I could tell them turn around."

"Yes, you could, it was a private jet." Everett opened the file and deftly changed the subject. "Your wife was poisoned with nicotine. Was she a smoker?"

"Monica? Hell no," Geoff said, outraged. "She was all about her body image."

"New boobs, lipo, chin implant, lip and nose

work." Everett didn't look up. "Yes, we see that from the work she had done."

"You're going to disparage a dead mother because she could afford plastic surgery?" Geoff said.

"Certainly not, all of that and being a mother," Lyra said calmly. "Except she didn't give birth to Bryce, did she? Who was his mother, Mr. Hart?"

She and Everett were always good at playing off each other, and she watched the color leech from Geoff Hart's face and his dark eyes shift away. It was the first crack in his perfect exterior. Gray suit that had to be worth a few hundred, neat haircut, clean shaven, and a four-thousand-dollar watch on his wrist. He didn't look like a man devastated about his wife being dead or his son missing.

"You are mistaken. Monica was Bryce's mother," he said stiffly.

"Oh, the coroner was pretty sure." Everett leaned back in his chair. "What did he say, Detective Temple?"

"His exact words were those hips and genitals had never seen a child pass through them," Lyra ad-libbed. "Which facility and doctor delivered him?"

"He was born overseas," Geoff answered.

Lie. Lyra didn't say the word, but she could tell his heart raced and tiny beads of sweat formed at his scalp.

"Interesting." Everett laced his fingers. "Did you have your wife killed, Mr. Hart?"

"I'll have your badge for that," Geoff snarled. "How dare you ask me such a thing?"

"Someone is always trying to take our badges," Lyra murmured and sat down. "Where were you when your wife was killed?"

Geoff turned his gaze on her. "I left for my office by six a.m. I had two procedures before I headed to the airport."

"You could have injected her with the nicotine and left. It takes a while to work," Everett jumped in.

"She would have symptoms fifteen minutes or so after being poisoned," Geoff pointed out. "If I poisoned her, she wouldn't have made it to the pool with Bryce."

Lyra looked at Everett then Geoff. "It is certainly interesting you know that fact."

"I work with people who fuck up their mouths smoking that shit and dental training didn't mean I don't need some medical training." Geoff was snide. "I have to know this stuff. She would have too much saliva in her mouth, nausea, dizziness, and her heart rate would slow… quickly."

Everett wrote on his note pad. "Thank you so much for that information. Lyra, does he sound like a murderer being a know-it-all and hiding it under the guise of medical training to you?"

Lyra sighed. "He surely does, and it doesn't explain how he and his wife are raising a son who seems to have been born via the miracle of magic."

"Immaculate conception?" Everett asked.

"No, that's when she created a baby without sexual intercourse," Lyra said.

Everett nodded. "Ah, got it."

Mr. Hart stood angrily. "Find my son and my wife's killer, detectives. The next time you talk to me, call my lawyer first."

"I'm sure we will have to," Everett said. They watched him leave before he asked, "What do you think?"

"He's lying and knows something, but is he a murderer? I doubt it," Lyra said. "His kind would worry about losing everything he worked for in prison."

"Doesn't mean he didn't hire someone to do it," Everett countered as he gathered up his notebooks and files.

Lyra stood. "Good point, so we should talk."

"I have a deposition about Tollie." Everett went back to being crisp and business like. "We'll get to that later."

"I'll run down birth records for Bryce, to make sure if he was lying about overseas, then follow up with the Amber alert and see if any processed evidence gave us anything," she said as they walked out.

"Yeah, do that."

Everett left without even a goodbye. She went to the desk that sat opposite his to work on the computer and add information to the case file. At some point someone dropped a manila envelope and a sandwich on her desk. She looked up and Louie stood there with a look of concern on his fac. Looking down at her watch, told Lyra it was well past lunch.

"Figured you should eat, since you're in the zone. It's from the food cart outside so it's good," Louie said. "Your partner seems in a mood."

Ah, it's a gossip offering, Lyra thought. She sniffed dramatically and decided to add fuel to the fire. "I don't know what's going on with him; it's like after we…. Never mind, thanks for the sandwich. What's the package?"

"It was dropped off downstairs for you, so I brought it up with lunch." Louie put his hand on her shoulder. "If you ever need to talk, I'm here."

"Louie, isn't delivering a package with no name kind of weird to you? Maybe it's anthrax or something," she said sweetly.

He shrugged. "Could be from your confidential informants, I don't know."

"One more thing, Louie," Lyra said and stopped his slow forward momentum. "How much is the pot for if me and Everett are fucking?"

His eyes widened for a moment then he bent to her ear. "Six hundred so far, and the odds are split down the middle. When you're ready to give me the scoop, I'll split it with ya."

"Do I seem to need three hundred dollars?" she asked.

Louie shrugged. "Then give it all to me, I don't care."

Lyra laughed. "Bless it, I love you, Louie. You don't give a fuck what you say to anyone."

He snorted and bit into his own sandwich as he walked away. Picking up the flat envelope before the sandwich, Lyra opened it. A blade of lilac grass fell out first. The color and scent… she was instantly on alert and looked around to see if anyone was watching before she saw the rest of the contents. It was one picture of her working the case at Monica's crime scene. She held the sash in her hand and was looking back as if staring directly into the camera. The caretaker had been there, close enough to take the picture, two simple words scrawled across the bottom in black. *Hello, Princess...*

Chapter Four

Shit, fuck, bless it… Lyra went through the list of curse words in her mind as she drove home that night. She worked late on the case, trying to focus and not think of the picture in her satchel and what she would do about it. She would call her uncle, for one, and since he was one of the Paladin Court, he of course would tell the others. How would she work around a warrior presence while doing her job? Lyra had no clue. Saying nothing was another option, but she knew that wouldn't happen. While she served the people of Tucson, she also had to protect Paladin because she was a dragon and it was home.

She wanted it all simple again, to work her case and not worry about her second nature until the urge to fly and be free took hold. Lyra stopped the car in her driveway and walked around the house to the back, leaving the side gate open. Her manicured lawn belied living in such a hot climate, and the lights in the pool beckoned her to sink into the water. She kicked off her shoes to let the warmth of the grass seep into her feet and her dragon almost purred in delight. She would have to appease her second nature soon because her stress in human form would agitate her second nature.

"Princess, time to come home."

She was so intent on trying to relax she didn't see the figures looming in the shadows of her awning until each grabbed her arms. Lyra stopped in her steps as they tried to drag her, and she was ready to defend herself. She sank into a squat causing both men to have to drop to bend at the waist. Lyra snapped her head back and caught one in the nose, and that made him let go. Her arm was free, and she punched the other one in the lower stomach before sweeping kick that took him off his feet. Lyra rolled away and was in a crouching position with her arms raised in front of her to protect her face but ready to fight. Her hair had come loose, and the long curls fell down her back and into her face. Within her dragon raged to be let loose.

"I will go nowhere. Who sent you?" Lyra demanded.

"Daughter of Hamon, you have been summoned by your father to denounce the ruling of the king about your betrothal," the guard said. "We will take you by force if necessary."

Lyra's smile was deadly. "I wish you would try."

"I wish you would too." It was Everett's voice. He had moved into her back yard. He walked wide semi circle with his gun trained on both men.

"She is the princess. No human will stop us from taking her!" One of her father's guards spat out.

"Since you look just as… human." Everett passed a quick look to her. "You are going to explain that comment. I think a bullet may do some damage to that body of yours."

Lyra stood tall. "Tell my father, I will not denounce the order of the king. It is my choice and do not come here again."

"This is so very weird," Everett murmured. "Listen to the… um… Princess or take a bullet."

Both men ran past her and jumped the back fence. She could hear their footfalls and then when they shifted to dragon form, the flap of wide wings. Everett heard none of this, but he slowly put his gun away while they silently assessed each other.

"So, I guess this is part of what you want to talk about," Everett commented. "Princess, huh?"

"Yeah part of it," she said slowly.

"So, family rich is royalty?" he asked.

"Yeah, sort of." Lyra shuffled her foot.

Everett snorted. "This conversation fills in so much, like how you got shot and seem basically fine and the princess thing."

"It's more of an I have to show you type thing." Lyra sighed in frustration and held out her hand. "Do you trust me?"

He looked at her hand, then her. "Is this a come with me if you want to live scenario?"

"Everett, do you trust me?" Lyra asked through gritted teeth.

"With my life," he answered honestly and put his hand in hers.

"Okay, come with me." She led him to her car.

He looked back as she dragged him along. "Don't you need your shoes?"

"Nope." She didn't look back. "We need the truck, though."

He kept looking at her while she drove, like all of a sudden, she had grown another head. What would he think when she gave her second nature free rein of her body? She wondered while she maneuvered the large Dodge truck out into the desert.

"Is this how royalty gets rid of people who know too much?" Everett laughed nervously. "You're not planning on planting me out in the rocks—at least bury deep enough so coyotes can't get me."

"You're being an idiot," she muttered.

Everett snapped back. "You haven't told me shit, Lyra, so excuse me about being nervous with all the secrecy going on."

"I know, I'm sorry. Trixie told me I should trust you, and I was scared…" she began.

"Hold the phone, Trixie knows?" Everett demanded to know. "Over me? That makes me feel better."

"I met Trixie when I was getting hell at the academy, and I was alone and away from home," Lyra explained. "I've known her longer than you and she's seen me naked."

"I've seen you naked," Everett pointed out.

"Good point. I knew her longer and she's my best friend," Lyra amended.

"Fine, I will give you that," he muttered.

Finally, she parked by an outcropping of rocks and slid from behind the driver's seat. It was a moment before Everett got out and slammed the door before coming around to where she stood looking up to the sky.

Lyra started speaking. "It's always so beautiful here… a sky full of stars…"

"What in the hell is going on?" Everett cut her off.

She turned and looked at him. "Bless it, I was getting to it… I'm a princess."

"Yeah, I got that from the guys trying to kidnap you," he said.

"But I'm not from here, not from earth, another place," she said gently.

He laughed incredulously. "So, you're an alien? Wait… you're not, are you?"

Lyra snorted. "Humans are so prideful. You think this vast universe and beyond and you are the only living thing. No, I am not an alien. I'm a dragon princess."

"Isn't that the definition of alien species?" Everett asked skeptically. "That is, if I believe you. If you don't want to tell me where you're a princess that's fine but we can't have people trying to kidnap you in the middle of every damn case… what are you doing?"

She had begun to take off her clothes. "You don't believe me, so I'll show you. Please don't be scared. I won't hurt you. I promise."

"I know you won't, I still have my gun on me," he answered.

Lyra took off the rest of her clothes and walked out farther where the earth was still warm under her feet. She gave herself over to her second nature, feeling it crawl along her skin pleasurably and control her entire body.

"The fuck…"

She heard Everett's words while her dragon took her body and she was completely changed. She looked down at her partner who was staring up at her form with his mouth open and yes, his gun drawn. She chuckled internally and it sounded like a guttural chuff. In this form a bullet wouldn't pierce her skin. Her dragon yowled in protest when she took control again and returned to human form. She walked towards Everett, and he stepped back looking at her in shock. There was no horror on his face, nor did he run so she counted that as a win.

She stopped moving. "Did… well, that's me."

"Couldn't shoot you, could I?" He put his gun away.

"No, did you want to shoot me?" Lyra asked

He shook his head. "No, but shit… you turned into a dragon in front of me. I have to wonder if I'm hallucinating."

"You weren't but there's much more I have to tell you." Lyra dressed and sat on a rock. "You want the truth, here is all of it."

He sat beside her and Lyra told him the story of her people and their protection of earth. She explained the last war and the Shen, even the caretakers and how they were disbanded for their treachery. He listened to the story of their lives and how they were connected to humans, either protected or mated. Lyra told him of her mother and why she came back to the earth realm. She didn't leave out why her father's guard tried to take her. He would hear it all, including how the sash may be connected to their case. Finally, she stopped talking and only the sound of night creatures calling to each other broke the silence as Everett digested it all.

"You have the picture they sent you back at your place?" he asked.

"No, I have it with me. I need to take it to London to the King's advisor," Lyra replied.

"You are so far away from London... Oh, portals?" Everett asked.

"Yes, that." She smiled. "If the caretakers are involved or kidnapping children, he has to know because they would track them way better than we could."

"This is our case," Everett practically growled.

"They want nothing to do with humans ever knowing they exist," Lyra said hurriedly. "Any information would be given to us."

"Unless it's the Shen things making an appearance again, then you kill them," he assessed and laughed as he dragged his hand through his hair. "Remember when the only thing we had to worry about was cops talking about us fucking?"

"That was this afternoon." She nudged shoulders with him. "The bet is up to six hundred dollars. Louie said if we give him the scoop, he'll split it."

Everett laughed. "We should admit it just for the payday."

"After telling you everything, do you still want to be my partner or is this all too weird and you can't trust me?" Lyra asked hesitantly.

"I can see why you didn't tell me this, because if you had told me when we first met, I would have had you institutionalized," Everett said. "I'm still pissed, especially because of getting shot. I don't care if you heal like a dream or you're bullet proof as a dragon, but you tell your partner when you get shot."

"I get that, and I am sorry for not coming clean earlier," Lyra said. "You and Trixie are the most important people to me outside my family."

"Who are in Texas and also dragons," Everett said.

"My uncle and one of my cousins. My aunt is human, and their daughter isn't," she explained. "The gene can be there or not. I could have been born without it. It may have been easier for my father to let go if I had been."

He covered her hand. "You are who you are meant to be. I had to learn that even with my asshole mother. It's not your father's right to tell you who you can and can't marry."

"I have to go if I want to be back here in time for work, if I have to go to Paladin. I will be late," she said apologetically.

"You've taken Trixie—can I go?" Everett asked hopefully.

"I'll ask for permission," Lyra smiled and teased. "You'll have to ride on my back to get there."

"You look sturdy enough, I'll deal," Everett teased.

She put her hands on her hips. "Are you saying I gained weight, Everett Craig?"

He held up his hands in defense. "No way, I would never say that to a woman let alone one who can change into a dragon. Can you breathe fire?"

"When need be yes, so don't piss me off," Lyra said wickedly. "Drive the truck back. Will you wait at the house, please?"

"Yeah, such a hardship waiting at your almost royal mansion with the pool and food." Everett walked back to the truck. "How will you get home?"

"We have our ways." She laughed. "I have a

dirt bike hidden out here for when I need it. I have the sash with me, in an evidence bag, so no one will contaminate it, but I have to show the king."

"Just make sure it's never out of your sight." Everett sighed. "I hope the Captain never gets wind of this or we are both screwed."

"I've spent years covering my ass with this secret. Even if he found out anything, I would take the hit," Lyra put her hand on his shoulder. "I would never do that to you, Ev."

"I know… This is all so very insane, me talking to a woman who turns into a dragon and has a hidden dirt bike."

She gave a husky laugh. "Thanks for trusting me."

Crazy. She heard him murmur to himself as he moved to the driver's side of the truck and got in. Lyra raised her hand in a wave as he pulled away before she took off her clothes and hid them for when she returned. Taking the form of her second nature again, she rose into the sky, happy to be free of the burden that came with keeping secrets from her partner. On impulse she dipped in the sky in front of the truck and let out a small stream of fire from deep in her throat. In her dragon form it amused her to see him swerve a little, but soon he controlled the truck and kept on his way.

She turned her mind to the task that followed, heading to her uncle and then they would go to London to see Hawke. If she had to go to Paladin to plead her case, then so be it, she was ready to take on a rogue caretaker sect, or to denounce her father and Dael. Lyra would handle both because she never backed away from a fight.

Ginna stayed with the children while she and her Uncle Kalv used the portals that took them to the London fortress of the Paladin dragons. It was the place where all the dragon wives and children were safely tucked away when the final battle of the war raged. It was also there the caretakers attacked and it was defended by seven wives who were not going to let themselves, or their children, be taken or used as pawns. She spoke to Hawke, the king's right hand, and explained her situation with her father and Dael. Then Lyra revealed the sash from the caretaker she'd taken from the evidence room for her case and showed him the picture.

It was decided then and there that Lyra would speak to the king and formally have her betrothal denounced in front of the court. This would nullify his ability to act on her behalf. Then in private the issue with the caretaker would be discussed. The latter came first, and Lyra knelt in front of the king who sat on his throne and seemed even larger than life when she was a child. The magic of Paladin kept him almost as young as she remembered except there was more silver hair at his temples. He grew his hair out and now it was on his shoulders and an untidy mass. Orin was not one for the pageantry of being royalty. He rolled his eyes when Lyra looked up from her position of honoring her king.

"Lyra, I have walked you around this palace and dragged you from under this very throne snooping and hiding. Stand up, will you?" Orin said with a smile on his face.

"My king," Lyra said formally, and he raised an eyebrow. "Sorry. Hey uncle Orin."

"That's better… look at you." Orin came down from the throne and lifted her in a hug that took her off her feet. "Earth realm suits you. Kalv tells me you are a kick-ass cop."

"Did he? Thanks." She glanced over to where her uncle and Hawke stood. They were all her uncles, not by blood but by the kinship they shared with him.

"Tell me," he said and led her to the large table where they had all eaten at some point in their lives. It was the centerpiece of the unity shared by the Paladin dragons, and it was only fitting that she spoke to them there.

"There are two issues," Lyra began and showed him the evidence bag. "The most pressing is the fact that I found this red sash at a crime scene where a mother was killed, and her son taken. Then this picture was sent to me at the precinct."

"Caretakers in the earth realm?" Orin looked at Kalv and Hawke. "You guys are there more often than not. Has our network heard anything?"

"Quiet on all fronts," Hawke answered, a hint of a British accent evident in his voice. It always made her smile because even though they resided in England, Daisey, his wife, never picked it up and her southern sweet voice stayed the same.

"We should send a contingent of warriors to Arizona..." Orin started, and she could see the king formulating a plan on how to protect his people and humans alike.

"Uncle Orin let me work this from the police angle," Lyra cut him off. "Sending a whole other layer of people, I cannot control just makes it worse. I can work the case and if I find anything that leads to the caretakers, I'll get word to Uncle Kalv and then the warriors can take care of it secretly."

"Skard and Iarl move with stealth," Orin pointed out.

Lyra looked at him skeptically. "Yes, a set of redheaded identical twins who hate human clothes and carry broad swords won't stand out. Please, I can do this. I went to earth realm to make a difference. Let me show you I can."

Orin was hesitant but then he nodded. "You have the point on this. Now what is the second issue, as if I didn't know."

"My father sent his guards to drag me home with the ridiculous idea it would cause me to marry Dael," Lyra answered. "I need a formal sanction at court."

Orin sighed. "Hamon won't be pleased."

"Uncle… my king, I am never going to marry Dael. Pardon my words, but he's a fucking asshole with greed and darkness within him," Lyra said. "We are not suited, and honestly I may end up shooting him if he keeps bothering me because he likes to grab me without consent."

Orin took a breath and his words were angry. "To do that is to act without honor. He cannot lead my warriors if this is his way."

Lyra ran her fingers over the granite of the table as she spoke. "My father has to understand that I am not going to return to Paladin or bend to his old-world views. I love the earth realm and it's my home just as much as Paladin. I feel my mother there and here; all there is with him is bitterness."

Orin stood with determination. "Send word to Hamon to come to the palace and convene the court."

"I'll tell my brother myself," Kalv's tone was somber and he turned to leave.

It took only an hour to convene the dragon court, which now took the recommendation of the court's wives as well. They fought for Paladin and Earth, so they too deserved a say. Lyra stood to the left of the throne and to the right was Dael and her father. His eyes widened when he saw her there, not with pleasant surprise but the shock of knowing it was she who asked for the court to be assembled.

"Hamon, you are here because your daughter has asked to have you forfeit from her life," Orin said loudly enough for everyone to hear. "Dael, you too are accused of taking liberties where one should not and off world, no less. Dael, you may answer first."

"She is to be my wife. I can go see my betrothed." Dael's voice held pride and he lifted his head.

"I am not yours," Lyra defended. "And is

grabbing me and pulling me against your naked body also a right?"

"Oh no he didn't," Raven, the wife of Raul, said in an outraged voice.

"Your father gave me the right," Dael said coldly.

Orin turned his attention to her father. Lyra looked at the man she barely knew. He was dressed regally in the royal colors of her people: burgundy and gold. He was always jealous of Kalv, for being a Paladin warrior and did not welcome him home after he was locked out of their realm. He didn't smile, there was no affection, the man who used to lift her high so the suns of Paladin could touch her face was cold and distant.

"What say you, Hamon?" Orin demanded.

"Lyra has forgotten the old ways," Hamon said. "Look at how she's dressed. This is not our way."

"We wives are all from that world and dress that way." Daphne was the mate to the twin warriors Skard and Iarl.

"If the royal warriors choose to dilute their line with humans, so be it," Hamon snapped condescendingly. "I learned my lesson with my own mistakes."

"That includes your queen," Orin's tone

became deadly. "I would suggest you rethink your next words wisely, before myself or my warriors choose to take offense."

Hamon snapped his mouth shut and took a moment before speaking again. "As her father with no mother to teach her the correct ways, it is my choice who she marries."

"The king can set that aside as he did. I want no part of marriage to Dael." Lyra almost shuddered in disgust. "Can he say with truth that he would honor a marriage with fidelity? His own words more than once are that he doesn't care for a marriage bed with me, only what comes from a union with the Hamon house."

"Do you deny her words?" Kalv asked. "And remember, I will know if you lie."

Dael had the good sense to think, and his eyes shifted in fear. Kalv always had a way of knowing things, it one was of the traits passed on to her. Plus he kept eyes on the new warriors of Paladin. He had eyes in the barracks and more.

"She speaks the truth, but I said those things in anger at her spurning of my affection," Dael answered.

"And you decide to take the portals to accost her," Queen Valencia mused. "Good to know."

"I ask my father be no longer allowed to speak on my behalf or control my holdings." Lyra was clear on what she was doing and knew it was finally time to end the obvious dislike her father had of her.

"She's always taken after her mother, and if she chooses this, there is no holdings to have, she forfeits it all," Hamon declared.

Hawke stepped forward. "You are incorrect. She is the child of a union with her mother. She is your blood and will have half of the Hamon holdings. When you die it all goes to her, the last of your line."

Hamon smiled coldly. "I could remarry and have another child."

"It would still be hers—she is first in your line," Hawke answered. "Until you die, then her choice is to give to this new wife and child born of spite."

Hamon looked at her Uncle Kalv. "You stand and let them treat me like this, brother?"

"You chose to treat your daughter, my niece, like meat, then you have no sympathy from me," Kalv answered calmly.

"All of you have been weakened by the lust of mortal female flesh," Hamon snarled.

Orin pulled his sword, the sound of mental against sheath echoed in the hall. Every person including Lyra gasped. His voice was cold. "Mind your tongue, lest I cut it from your head. You leave here with lands and your pride, but not much else."

"Give me my freedom, Father," Lyra implored. "Then you can be done with me and the curse you said my mother was."

"Do it of your own volition or have it done for you," Orin said simply.

Hamon turned to her. "You are now not my concern. I no longer call you my daughter."

Somehow it didn't feel as bad as it should have when he said the words.

"You stopped calling me that long ago," Lyra answered.

"Dael, consider your standing as a warrior of this court, the men and women you lead," Orin said. "As before, the betrothal between you and Lyra of the house of Hamon has been nullified. You are to leave her in peace. If you do not, or we receive word of any other acts that are not of our ways, our honor, then we shall act accordingly."

Dael bowed low. "My king, I understand, and I will not fail you again."

"See that you don't," Orin said. "Lyra, we are preparing the evening meal. Will you join us?"

"I will, thank you, my king," Lyra answered.

That was his way of telling Dael and Hamon he was done with them. With a nod, Dael turned and left while her father threw her a disgusted look before he spoke.

"Just like your mother, and you will end as such," Hamon said.

"Luckily, that is no longer your concern," she said. "Goodbye, father."

He walked out of the great hall, and she knew that she would never see him again. With the formality over, Lyra was left to get re-acquainted with the dragon warriors and their wives. She had grown looking up at all of them with adoration, wishing she could be one of them to be away from her father for a while. Then her Uncle Kalv took her, and Lyra was finally able to see how her mother lived and the stories she told.

She felt one weight of her shoulders only to be the replaced by the one that would not be part of her case. Were the caretakers somehow involved with Monica's death and taking Bryce? Who was the child's mother, if not her? There was more under the surface and she would have to peel back the layers to the truth. To protect this world and the one she now called home, she would find the answers.

Chapter Five

The working theory was that the surrogate who gave birth to Monica's son wanted the child back and killed her in the midst of a kidnapping. That didn't sound right to Lyra. Why would Geoff Hart get so defensive unless there was more to hide? She came back from Paladin with a host of questions and not many answers. At least that part with Dael and her father had been closed, and she hoped permanently.

She wondered if she was a bad daughter for not caring that her father would no longer be in her life. He drew the battle lines long before she understood the war. Either choose him, be the dutiful daughter and forget her mother, or be her own woman and face his disdain. In the end, she made the right choice. Lyra now had to focus on the case and find out how the caretakers were involved.

Everett drove the car through the city the evening after she came home. They were going back to the beginning and heading toward the apartment complex where Monica was murdered. Monica's husband wouldn't talk to them, but maybe the best friend could open up some doors on who the baby's mother was. While he merged and passed traffic seamlessly, Lyra thoughts drifted to when she got back from Paladin that night. He'd slept in her guest room after they spent hours talking and she explained her life and how she ended up in the earth realm.

"You're saying your mother was human and your father hated her for it," Everett asked. "Then why did he sleep with her?"

"It was the novelty, I guess," Lyra shrugged. "Come to earth, taste the local flavors, and then go back home. Except my mom got pregnant, and he took her to Paladin and expected her to be something she was not. She worked her whole life and now he expected her to sit and look pretty, dutiful, and submissive. I think I take after her, strong willed."

"How did she die?" Everett asked gently.

"They had an argument one night and my mother ran off, furious. She told him she was taking me and going back to earth. She still had her life there," Lyra repeated the story in a monotone. Pretending it happened to someone else was how she had learned to cope with it all. "I was ten, and I heard him yelling for her and then her scream. Our house faced the falls—she fell over the end onto the rocks and into the darkness. I often wonder if he had her pushed."

"That's fucked up." Everett sat back and took a gulp of his beer. "He's the type of man to kill your mother?"

She raised an eyebrow in his direction. "He sent his guards to get me by force."

"Touché," he murmured. "Your king put a stop to all that, I assume?"

"He did." She drank from her own beer. "My father no longer can act on my behalf. He tried to leave me destitute but when he took my mother as wife, half was hers and that is mine. My uncle Kalv would never let me do without so I wasn't concerned."

"Now what?" Everett asked.

She looked at her partner. "We solve the case and find out if and why the caretakers are here."

"And if these caretakers are involved and we find them?" Everett posed the question. "They can't go to trial, can they?"

She looked away and shook her heard. "My kind would send warriors to take care of the issue. Hawke, his second, would make it all disappear."

"Tied up in a neat little bow," Everett said, and she heard a hint of bitterness in his voice.

"Listen, I understand if this is too much, the

secrets and… I can ask for a transfer after this," Lyra said hesitantly.

Everett leaned forward and pointed at her. "No ma'am, you don't get to introduce me to this life and then walk away. I may not like the tactics, but I have to understand it. After all you told me, people would freak the fuck out. I'll deal but hopefully this is the first and last time I need to hear about this kind of shit in any investigation we are a part of."

"From your lips to the God's ears," she murmured.

"These gods, like Odin and all that shit, they are real huh?" Everett questioned.

"That's our creator—well, part of me anyway," Lyra explained.

"You know you scared the shit out of me when you breathed fire in the sky, right?"

His comment was nonchalant, but they looked at each other and began to laugh. It was then she knew it was okay, they would be fine. After a comfortable silence, she sank into her own thoughts and when the car came to a stop, it pulled her from her reverie.

"Thought you fell asleep on me there," Everett said. "Aren't you supposed to have more stamina being a dragon and all?"

"I need sleep," Lyra grumbled. "We talked

until three a.m. and then were at the desk at eight in the morning. From there we went through phone record, financials, looked for secret bank accounts, and tried to figure out if she had a surrogate. We asked for a warrant to get Geoff's DNA and sample from the child's brush to see if he was the father. His lawyer got that shot down. We had a half a sandwich for lunch and canvassed Monica's favorite hangout spots. I'm running on fumes and I'm hungry."

"Fine, after this we can eat." Everett chuckled. "One thing for sure, dragon or not, when a woman is hungry, she gets cranky."

She patted his shoulder as they walked through the front doors of the complex. "You learn quickly."

"It will have to be a quick meal, I have a date tonight," Everett announced. "Carmen is not one you want to keep waiting."

Why did that comment rub her the wrong way? Lyra bit the inside of her lip as they stepped in the elevation. In irritation, instead of replying she took it out on the button to the fifth floor and mashed it hard with her finger. After all she shared, they were closer, and it seemed like just another day to him. *I don't care who he takes to dinner as long as I get my food first,* she told herself firmly. He whistled a soft tune as they moved upwards and then the sleek doors opened silently to reveal royal blue carpet that was exclusive to that luxurious complex.

They walked to Amy's door and she knocked. Lyra expected to at least find her husband home. But it was her and the baby alone again. She was clearly tired and had puffy eyes that showed she had been crying on and off for at least for a few days.

"Amy, how are you?" Lyra sensed the woman's fragile condition. "This is my partner, Everett Craig. I'm sorry if it's late and we are interrupting dinner."

"No, it's fine, it's just me and the baby," she said quietly.

"Your husband not home?" Everett asked.

She shook her head. "No, he works late… a lot. They all do."

Amy stepped back and ran her hand over her hair. In the bouncer sat her daughter chewing on her hand as it bounced to comfort her from crying. She was upset but Amy was dressed this time around in casual jeans and a jersey shirt from one of the Arizona colleges. Her computer sat open on the coffee table and a stack of papers were neatly to the side.

"Did we interrupt work?" Lyra asked.

"Not really," Amy answered. "I was working

on my thesis, trying to keep my mind off… stuff. You guys can sit down if you like."

"Can we ask you a few questions?" Everett sat in an armchair while Lyra took the loveseat and reached out so the baby could grab her fingers.

"Sure, go ahead, but I don't know much anything past what I told you," she answered.

"Who was Bryce's mother?" Lyra asked and whatever color that Amy had in her face bled away. She spoke gently. "Don't lie, Amy. The coroner already told us Monica never had a child. If we are going to find him, we need your help."

Tears slid down Amy's cheeks. "He's mine, and Geoff is the father."

Lyra looked up at Everett in shock. This was a stunner and neither of them expected that. *What the hell is going on in this place?*

"Explain this to us," Everett encouraged.

"Our husband's work late and are in very high-powered jobs." Amy took a breath. "When we moved here, we got into a lifestyle pretty quickly. This building is filled with swingers."

"So, you share partners?" Lyra asked for clarification.

Amy nodded. "I knew Monica from college. She was a few years ahead of me so when we needed a place she suggested moving here. Geoff had an eye for me almost instantly, and as you can see, David is hardly around. He liked the thought of it, being able to fuck someone without it being called cheating. Sometimes we had a foursome, or he'd watch me, and Geoff and I would watch David and Monica."

"Okay," Lyra said the word slowly, waiting for Amy to continue.

"It went past that for Geoff. He fell for me and I love my husband," Amy said and looked at them with wide eyes. "It's just sex, but I love my husband with all my heart. I got pregnant and that was unexpected, but it worked out because Monica wanted a baby but didn't want to carry one. She was into her body image."

"They took the baby to raise as their own, and David was okay with it because it wasn't his kid," Everett assessed.

"And I was close by to see my son grow up," Amy added. "It was a good arrangement, but Geoff wanted me all to himself. The last few months, he's been trying to get me to leave David and we'd take the kids before leaving Arizona."

"And you said no,'' Lyra surmised.

Amy swiped at the tears on her cheeks. "I told David and that was it, for both of us. It wasn't fun anymore; it was going to break up marriages. We were planning to move. I told Monica, so we could make plans so I could see Bryce. No matter what, we both loved him, and I wanted to be in his life even if she was his mother."

"Let me guess, Geoff found out," Lyra murmured.

"I don't know!" Amy cried and her baby started to fret. She shushed her daughter and calmed her voice. "But then you told me Monica is dead and Bryce was gone. I can't leave without him! You have to find him for us! David and I talked, and we'll raise the both but…" She sobbed and took a shuddering breath. "I'm scared that Geoff did something…"

"Has he reached out to you to say Bryce is okay or to make any demands?" Everett asked.

Amy shook her head no. "I went over there to beg him to give me Bryce if he had him and I wouldn't say a word. He tried to play it off like he knew where my baby was, and I wanted to see him. I needed to let him take me right there." She shuddered in disgust. "I could tell he was lying, and I don't feel… he… I got out of there and came back here."

If Lyra disliked Geoff Hart before, she despised him now. Amy implored them with her hands. "I'm begging you to find my baby, please, find Bryce."

Lyra stood and took her hand before promising. "We will, I swear it."

They left soon after, and she hoped her words calmed the young mother. As she and Everett walked back to the elevator, they discussed the new information.

"Seems Geoff had more to hide than we thought," Everett said as they waited for the doors to open.

"Kill his wife, hide the baby, and force Amy to be with him," Lyra said. "Seems we have a man who would do anything to get what he wants."

"We can't bring him right in. We don't know where he could have the baby stashed," Everett pointed out. "But we can have another conversation with him and his lawyer. Let's see if we can shake his composure."

They got on the lift and headed back to the lobby.

"We need to get eyes on him twenty-four seven. Maybe he'll lead us to Bryce and whoever is helping him," Lyra suggested.

"Can't hurt. At least we can say with at least seventy percent certainty the baby is okay," Everett commented. "They won't come in until the morning, his lawyer will make sure of that, so we'll grab you a meal and I'll head to my date."

Lyra faked a smile. "You know what? Drop me off at Trixie's place and I'll grab some pub food there. We have plans anyway." *It's a lie but he won't know the difference.*

"You sure?" Everett gave her a sidelong look. "You were grumpy as hell a minute ago."

"I'm sure, drop me off and go get your jollies," she said as they got into the car.

She focused on the case and not the fact that now his love life was bothering the hell out of her. What they learned tonight didn't tell her why she found a caretaker sash at the crime scene and who was watching her. The more they unraveled, the more complicated the case seemed to be. *Bless it, I need a drink.*

Drink number two made her shoulders relax but she was still glum. She swirled the cherry in the top of the amber liquid in her rocks glass. *What is wrong with me?* Lyra wondered. *Why do Everett's dating habits matter all of a sudden? When did he stop being a buddy and become someone more attractive, and how did I not see it happening?*

"Any answers in that glass?" Trixie commented with a smile.

She came down the bar to grab empty plates. The first thing she did was to get a dinner menu and order two chicken wing specials that came with fries and coleslaw.

"Damn woman, I wish I could eat like you and still look like that," Trixie exclaimed.

"High metabolism, because of… you know." Lyra held up two fingers.

Trixie put the plates in the bussing tub and placed it under the bar. "Why so glum, chum?"

"This is your fault." Lyra pointed at her. "Telling me to share my secret with Everett for one and telling me he was interested in ways other than being my partner."

"Um, first off I think Ev seeing the two guards coming to drag you away is the what put the kibosh on your secret," Trixie pointed out. "And if that switch flicked in your head then it's because you finally feel free to think like that."

"I told him the truth, he saw me in my true form, and it's like another day of the week." Lyra sighed. "Maybe the dragon part was too much. We aren't the prettiest things in nature."

"Thank god this place is half empty and you're so far down this side." Her friend laughed. "They'd wonder what you were drinking to see dragons."

"Am I being loud?" Lyra asked in surprise.

Trixie chuckled. "No, I'm messing with you."

"Cash me out, please. I am going home to

take a swim then wallow in self-pity until I pull myself out of it." Lyra stood and pulled out her money clip from her pocket while Trixie went to the point of sale system at the corner of the bar. "How much do I owe you?"

"Two whiskeys with cranberry, two wing specials… thirty-five dollars and twenty-two cents," Trixie answered.

Lyra gave her a fifty-dollar bill. "See you in a few days?"

"You know where to find me unless you mean a shopping trip because I'm in," Trixie said brightly.

"Ugh, you know I'm trying to break myself of the addiction… Tuesday?"

"Tuesday it is." Trixie winked.

Lyra waved and walked down the alley beside the bar. She had what she considered a small penchant for shopping and lacy underthings. Two months was a good run and after the past week she deserved some shopping therapy. She'd heard the way men talked about her in the precinct; she was pretty and tall, but she was a cop and sometimes seemed too masculine. She beat them all out in training, in weapons, even the required certifications or three-mile run. Carrying a purse wasn't practical—a dragon flying through the air with a Gucci purse in its mouth was not going to be Lyra.

The heels and sexy dresses stayed in the closets because she didn't date, and the club scene wasn't something she frequented. The few times Trixie begged her to be wing man showed Lyra that she would never date someone she met in a club. So, the side of her that she considered sexy stayed hidden away.

The footsteps fell into a rhythm behind her after she passed the cross streets and under the streetlights. People were out for the evening, but this person blended in behind her quickly and trailed her every step. She picked up speed, pretending to look at her phone as she walked, and the pace of her new shadow increased as well. She slowed to a stop and muttered at her phone as if getting an annoying message, and the footsteps stopped as well. Lyra scanned the surroundings before crossing the street to a small, familiar park. Fewer people on the street with a tree line; it was the perfect place to find out who her new friend was.

Walking with her hands in her pocket, Lyra suddenly made a quick move and ducked into the park. She used the dimness of the night and the shadows of the trees to blend into the darkness quickly. As expected, her shadow ran past, wondering where she had gone, and she assessed the back of the person wearing a dark hoodie as they searched the path ahead for her.

Lyra stepped out of the shadows. "What do I have that you could possibly want?"

The assailant turned around and she only got a glimpse of the face, male… before he started to run. Lyra gave chase and slowly gained until she hurled herself at his back and took the man down to the ground. That should have ended it, but this person surprised her. With a deft scissor kick that sent her hurtling through the air and a flip, he was solidly on his feet.

The attack was on, and she deftly defended the blows that came at her with precision, showing this person was trained in martial arts, but so was she. One flat palm against the hooded chest sent her assailant stumbling away from her. Lyra was on the attack now, and as she rushed forward, she managed to get his right arm trapped and was about to take out the knee with a downward kick. She inhaled in victory and her eyes widened in surprise.

"Dragon?" she whispered in surprise.

"Hey, what's going on down there? I'm calling the cops!"

A jogger tore her attention away, and she turned her head to the voice. It was all her attacker needed. She felt the hit connect to her jaw and the pain bloomed through her face. Oh, that was a dirty trick because she knew the feel of brass knuckles as she went to her knees.

"Later Princess," the guttural voice said, and she heard the footsteps run away while she tried to regain her equilibrium.

She got to her feet, rubbing her jaw, as the jogger ran up. "Are you okay? Oh my god, I have my cellphone I'll call the police."

"No need to, I'm the police. That was a pickpocket I was chasing." Lyra took the badge from her jacket pocket and showed the young woman and lied. "I've got people on scene; they'll catch him on the other side."

The woman shook her head and her ponytail danced from side to side. "I swear it's getting worse and worse around here. Thank you, though. It makes me feel safer that the police are around."

"That's our job, ma'am. You be careful while you finish your run."

The young woman nodded and jogged in the opposite direction. Lyra smoothed her hand over her jaw that was sore, and her irritation rose. Definitely a dragon but brass knuckles was a low blow and told her while they had some skill, he was still weak. She was thinking youngling but why try to oust her and why were they on the earth realm?

"Later indeed," Lyra murmured, knowing this was far from over. "I have your scent now. I have your fucking scent."

Leaving the park, she used the app on her phone to get a car service to pick her up. Usually when she let Everett use the car, she either took the scenic route from her secure location and went home in dragon form. Or he took her home first so she could grab another one of her rides and she went on her merry way. There was no way she was flying home, not after this. Her assailant was unknown and there could be more involved. Being watched was a high possibility so ride share it was. Stepping into her home, she took off her coat with a deep sigh and threw it on the cream-colored leather sofa.

Lyra walked to her wine cabinet, poured herself a glass of wine, and sipped at the rich, bold merlot. She was swirling the drain in her depression—the attack from some unknown fucking dragon and everything for the past week bothered her. *I need pretty therapy,* she thought suddenly and did something she always loved when a pick-me-up was absolutely necessary. She took the remote from the coffee table and started her music before going to her bathroom and filling the tub with hot, scented water.

Soaking for an hour definitely changed her

disposition, and Lyra got pretty with a red, skintight dress and expensive heels. She studied her reflection in the mirror, seeing her beauty and wondering why men focused only on her strength as a turn off. Trixie said human men made strong women feel like it was a curse to be able to handle their business. That was one part of living in the earth realm she didn't like because on Paladin women like her were revered. *Will I have to find a man back home?* she wondered and then looked on her bed as the chimes of her phone went off. Lyra frowned at the number. Why would work be calling now?

"Temple here," she answered briskly.

"Hey, Temple, you need to come get your partner from the office," Louie's familiar voice came over the line.

"Why would I need to come to the precinct to get Everett?" Lyra asked dryly. "He works there too. Maybe he stopped in before his date to work."

"You'd think, expect he's semi-drunk at his desk raging about the asshole demon," Louie explained. "I figured I should call you before brass catches wind and sends him for a psych eval."

His mother, oh shit. "Okay, I'm on my way."

She hung up thinking she should change but

then decided against it. *Fuck them,* she thought and got the keys to her new sports car. *I am not hiding myself for anyone, not anymore.* It took twenty minutes before she parked the sleek machine in front of the precinct and the engine purred to a stop. Police coming in and out stopped and stared at her baby, then their mouths dropped when they saw it was her.

"Jesus, Temple, that your car?" Stanley, one of the detectives on night, looked her up and down. "Um… you… you clean up."

"Yes, it is, and thank you I guess," Lyra answered. "I didn't know I looked like a dreg before."

"No, no," Stanley said hurriedly. "You look regular, you know, like jeans and stuff, I mean ordinary."

Lyra raised her eyebrow. "Ordinary…"

He ran his hand through his hair. "You look good, okay."

"Thank you, Stan." Lyra walked inside.

It wasn't any different when she went inside. Mouths dropped from both men and women officers and the desk Sargent dropped his pen. She took the elevator upstairs to the floor where they worked. It had a range of nicknames from Detective Den to Bullpen, but it was shared by day and night shift investigators. She walked in with a slew of whistles from the nightshift boys and Louie choked on his coffee.

"You all are children," Lyra said, shaking her head.

"You can come to work dressed like this anytime," Louie said. "Who knew you could look like that?"

"Seriously, Louie? The way you guys are acting would make anyone think I dress like a gremlin in jeans," Lyra said in irritation.

Louie shrugged. "I always told ya a little make-up never hurt nobody. Now look, I'm right. Men like to see some eye candy."

"And women like to be able to see a man's dick, not play hide and seek for it." Lyra looked down to his stomach.

He pointed at her. "You're right, but I love donuts more than sex at this point in my life. Your partner is over there. I gagged him on some coffee."

"Thanks Louie." Lyra looked over to where his head was on the table. "Lieutenant isn't here, is he?"

"Nah, he had plans. Get him out of here, will you?" Louie asked, walking away. "God knows I don't want to play nursemaid to a cop who's coo-coo for cocoa puffs."

Lyra moved to the desk and placed her hand

on Everett's shoulder. "Hey Ev, shouldn't you be on a hot date?"

He looked up and his eyes widened. "Hell, were you?"

"I was out," she said thinking it sounded more plausible than doing it to feel better at home.

He waved her away. "Well get back to it, I'm fine."

"You're obviously not," Lyra said gently. "Come on, you can take a swim at my place, clear your head. I can get pizza delivered."

"Nah." He put his head on the desk.

"Everett, get your ass up," Lyra ordered.

"Fine, you're too pretty to be such a hardass," he muttered.

She didn't say a word as she walked out of the bullpen with him trailing behind her. He got into the passenger side of the Bugatti without a word and not even a question to drive it. His mother had to have pulled a number on him. Lyra got in, started the car, pulled out and merged slowly into traffic.

"Want to tell me what's going on?" Lyra asked gently.

"Carmen, well she turned out to be the daughter of my mother's friend," Everett said. "Sent to bullshit and fuck me into submission of what my mother wants."

"You are kidding me, right?" Lyra said.

"Oh, I wish I was," Everett said. "But she had a slip, mentioned that place where my mom lives. After an interrogation and some tears, she let me know my mother promised Carmen and her mother ten thousand dollars if they could get me to sign over my father's place to her."

"No fucking way. Why does she want your dad's place?" Lyra kept her eyes on the road as she maneuvered traffic back to her house.

"It's not for sentiment. She was the cause of my dad killing himself, to escape that witch the man got me to eighteen and out of the house before he ate a bullet." Everett's tone held anger and pain. "She wants to sell the farm and the 100 acres of land to a developer. Even in the end, my dad made sure she didn't win. He left his entire estate to me. It's not much, but that ranch would catch her a pretty penny."

"She and my dad could never meet, it would start the apocalypse," Lyra teased.

Everett chuckled. "Thanks for that. I don't get it. I barely talked to that woman for the last fifteen years, and she is still trying to fuck up my world. And every damn time she tries something, it just brings back the fact..." He cleared his throat. "The fact that my dad loved me enough to stay around as long as he could, but for a sliver of peace, she drove him to his death."

"I'm sorry Ev." Lyra covered his hand with her, and he squeezed. "You got me and if you ever need me, you know I'm here… for anything."

"I know, partner." Everett looked over at her. "Best partner, best buddy I ever had."

Buddy. The word settled over her like a wet blanket and the rest of the drive home was silent. At the house, she let them both inside and went to the kitchen and ordered pizza from her favorite gourmet place.

"I ordered the pizza, and there are swim trunks in one of the bedrooms." Lyra waved her hand down the hall. "You know where everything is."

"You not staying up and eating with me?" Everett asked.

She shook her head, feeling suddenly emotional. "I've had a long day; I'm going to go to bed and veg out until the TV puts me to sleep."

"You okay?" Everett's voice held concern.

"Yeah, I'm fine…" Suddenly she couldn't keep her feelings to herself any longer. "No, I'm not. Everett, look at me. Why is it that all you or anyone sees is a buddy? For a minute there, after the shooting and Trixie's place and me sharing my secret, I thought we'd be closer. But then you saw past me and went to this Carmen chick. Granted, she turned out to be a plant for your mom, but why is it so easy to overlook me as just a good cop, partner or buddy?" She looked at him. "Why couldn't you see me as more, did my… my second nature scare you? Am I ugly because of it?"

Lyra didn't know what to expect, and she was scared of his answers. Did she take it too far and ruin whatever relationship they could have? She couldn't not be strong. It was part of her nature just like her dragon. Everett didn't say a word. Instead, he strode toward her and took her lips in a kiss that almost buckled her knees. He walked her backwards briskly until she felt the wall and his tongue delved into her mouth. Lyra made a kitten-like noise, one she never thought could escape her. He pinned her hands over her head and continued to assault her senses with a searing kiss that made her hot and wet all at once.

Everett looked down at her. "I can see your mind racing, thinking maybe it's the alcohol I had or a moment of weakness my mother caused. So, I'll be clear now. When you crawled out of bed naked, I wanted to forget we had a job and fuck you right there. When you said you were a virgin, I made the decision no other man would ever take you."

Lyra held her breath as he spoke, and she stared up into his face. She saw so much there, from blatant desire to something more, and Lyra couldn't understand it.

"Trying to work out in my head how to be your partner and your lover has been on my mind for a long while," Everett continued. "I don't want to mess this up because you are a damn good cop. But I fucking go to sleep rock hard for you every night. And all those dates that I claim to be on never happen. I'm home thinking about you."

"Then why?" Lyra asked.

"Because I've seen cops lose themselves in relationships that happen in precincts and I've seen the side effects of those that don't end well," he answered. "We aren't going to be the latter."

"Then what are we going to do?" Lyra looked at his lips, wanting him to kiss her again.

As if sensing her need, Everett kissed her long and hard before answering. "You are going to go to bed before I peel that dress off you and leave the heels on. And we'll revisit this again when we both aren't raw from the night. We'll go day by day and build something solid."

"I like the sound of that," Lyra said. "But to be clear, you want me?"

Everett kissed her and chuckled. "Yes, you nut, even though I'm older than you."

"Don't worry about that," she said when he moved away. "Dragons age at a way slower rate than humans. You'll see when I take you to Paladin, it will affect you too."

"Another perk," he said. "Now go to bed. Remember, we are taking it slow."

"Night, Everett." Lyra suddenly felt very light, like she didn't need her wings to fly.

"Hey Lyra," he said, and she turned before heading into the hall.

"Yes?"

He kicked off his shoes. "I'm glad you weren't on a date tonight; I'd have had to shoot him."

Lyra laughed. "What if it was a her?"

"Same thing." He sat down and took up her remote.

She laughed as she went down the hall to get changed and wondered how this new path in their relationship would work out. In the end, she left the pizza on the counter because he had fallen asleep on the couch. Lyra covered him with a blanket and brushed his hair away with soft fingers. Her night had turned out to be not bad at all. She rubbed her jaw that barely hurt right now. She'd have to tell him about the incident in the park tomorrow. *He's gonna flip his lid.*

Chapter Six

Was it weird that she felt more alive when they were sitting in the bland interrogation room? But this was in her area, the place she could catch them in deceit, and it was all on record. They didn't say anything else about last night, not even the kiss. She'd hoped there would've been another in the morning, but his smile when they took her truck into the precinct was definitely different.

It sent a warm thrill into her gut as they drove into work. Now they sat across from Geoff Hart who looked a bit more haggard than last time even though his charcoal gray suit was immaculate. Next to him sat his lawyer, the epitome of a shark in a suit. The long, pinched face and angry eyebrows were meant to put fear in his opponent. Lyra chuckled unexpectedly and everyone looked at her.

"Oh, I'm sorry." Another laugh escaped her. "I don't mean to laugh, but you look like one of those cartoon characters they draw for tourists that exaggerate features. And it's exactly like, a taller version of that short cartoon cowboy that's on TV."

Everett laughed out loud. "Yeah, I see it now."

"Are we here to disparage my appearance or speak to my client?" His lawyer's voice was droll.

Lyra sighed in humor and then her smile left instantly. "Let's talk. Tell us where Bryce is, Geoff."

"My client doesn't know where the boy is," the lawyer answered.

Everett sat back. "I thought we were talking to him. Especially now we know Amy Pascal is Bryce's mother, and he's been trying to get her to leave her husband and run off with him."

"Did your client tell you about the little swingers club they have going on in their ritzy apartment complex?" Lyra laced her fingers together. "Amy is frantic about her son, you could at least put her mind to rest, Geoff. What kind of monster kills the only mother his child knows trying to get another woman?"

Geoff slammed his hand on the metal table. "I don't have Bryce! Don't you think I want to see my son?"

"Not really, because right now, he was a weapon to hurt the woman who spurned you,"

Everett snapped. "She doesn't want you, sex was sex to her, but you had to take it to another level."

"What is it the millennials say, you had to… 'catch feelings'?" Lyra asked.

Geoff leaned his head back and closed his eyes before righting himself and looking at them. "Yes, I didn't love Monica anymore, yes I wanted Amy to leave David and take off with me. But I don't have it in me to kill anyone and I'm dying with the fact that my son isn't home sleeping in his own bed."

"Amy wants her son too. When he's found, she's going to ask for custody." Lyra watched for his reaction and got what she was looking for—his composure crumbled.

"Bryce is my son, mine. I won't have that spineless fool she married raise him," Geoff raged.

She prodded further. "Seems to me he couldn't be that spineless if she chose him over you. He must be the better man, better father, if your money couldn't even sway her."

"Amy is young and doesn't know what the hell she wants, but when she sees I'm the right man…" Geoff's lawyer covered his hand so his client would stop talking.

"You're going to show her, right?" Everett's tone was crisp. "By any means necessary? You really think she will want a man who more than likely murdered his wife and is hiding his own son?"

"All you have is conjecture and unless you're arresting my client, it's time for us to leave." The lawyer stood and urged Geoff to his feet.

"Longer that baby is gone, the more it looked like you killed your wife… and your child," Lyra said.

His reaction was pure horror, and his lawyer practically had to push him out of the room.

"If he killed his wife, Bryce is still alive," Lyra murmured. "You can't fake a reaction like that."

"He won't hurt a kid, but he'll hold one as a hostage to get a woman," Everett replied. "Yeah, I still think he's a douche."

"I do too. The tail will be on him and we can see where he goes," Lyra said. "We should stake him out tonight, see if we caused him to have ghost sensations."

"You mean spooked him?" Everett laughed as they left the room. "Jesus, that one got me. Yeah, let's take over around six tonight and see if he gets froggy."

Lyra checked her phone and frowned. "My uncle left me a message. Said he's in town and needs to see me."

"Want me to hold down the fort?" Everett asked.

Lyra texted back quickly and spoke as she did. "No, you can go with me if you want, he won't mind."

"He won't eat me, will he?" Everett teased softly looking around.

"Screw with his niece and he just might." Lyra laughed. "Come on,

We're going to meet him at Noodle-Noodle, he's hungry."

"It's not even noon yet," he said following her. "How much does your family eat, anyway?"

Lyra snorted. "Wait until you come to a festival on Paladin and there's a great feast then ask me that question again."

"Are there bare-breasted wenches, like the movies." Everett leaned over the car. "I mean, I can look away and all, since you people seem so free with nudity."

Lyra rolled her eyes. "Why does it always have to be some pagan woman with large breasts that human males go to as a visual?"

"Freud would say we are fixated on our mothers." Everett bounded down the steps. "Driver?"

"Passenger." She held out her hand and he threw her the keys. "I read Freud. He is a perverted nitwit; some good ideas but incestuous thoughts to say the least."

"I agree," he answered.

Noodle-Noodle was an old laundromat that had been turned into a restaurant to suit the new gentrification of that area. Gone were the check-cashing businesses, pawn shops, and dollar stores. It was replaced by little WiFi coffee shops, a hot yoga studio, wine and paint and various vegan eateries. At least the Asian fusion restaurant where they were meeting her uncle had meat options. Telling a dragon his food would consist of veggies, broth, and noodles may cause an unwanted fire. Within fifteen minutes they were seated across from her very formidable uncle. She was eighteen when the final war happened, and two years later living with them in the earth realm. In ten years, he hadn't gained but a few wrinkles around his eyes and some gray at his temples. He was standing outside when they walked up, and Everett eyed her uncle warily.

"Are all your people that massive?" he questioned in a low voice.

"They're tall, but the court of Paladin warriors are larger than most." Lyra's voice held humor.

"Well Jesus, I'm tall and I still feel like a fucking dwarf," he muttered.

Lyra was amused by his words. She was pulled into her uncle's large embrace as soon as she stood in front of him and almost smothered against his broad chest. Because of Ginna, he seemed more comfortable in regular human clothes. He wore a t-shirt that stretched across his chest and dusty jeans. The dragons had a soft spot for biker boots and his were covered in dust.

"Hey youngling." He looked down at her fondly.

She smiled up at him. "Uncle Kalv, this is Everett Craig, my partner.

Everett held out his hand. "Nice to meet you, Sir."

Kalv raised an eyebrow. "Sir? I like that, a polite young man."

Lyra slapped at her Uncle's shoulder. "Stop that, you both could be the same age."

Kalv grinned. "How old are you, Everett Craig?"

"Just Everett," he answered. "I'm thirty-five."

"Well, Everett Craig, I am a few hundred years older than you, so to me you are a young man." Kalv turned and opened the door. "Shall we eat?"

"Should I tell him, just to call me Everett... again?" her partner asked.

Lyra shook her head. "It won't make a difference, it's a thing they do."

"So how old can you guys get?" Everette found them a table and pulled out the chair for her in a gallant manner.

Kalv sat and spoke as he studied the menu. "Thousands of years. Human aging is slowed considerably in Paladin, so our wives never look like they've aged."

"So, you'll be thousands of years old?" Everett asked Lyra.

She shrugged. "I'm half human, so that depends on how much time I spend in Paladin."

"How are you and your people not a National Geographic documentary?" Everett said amazed.

Kalv looked up and his look was deadly. "Because those who know of us know to keep our secret lest they become a meal."

Everett gulped. "Understood."

"Great, Uncle Kalv. I finally convinced him we wouldn't eat him and there you go." Lyra grinned.

"I haven't eaten a human in years," Kalv answered.

Everett looked from one to the next and snorted. "Thanks for teasing the human guy."

Kalv was chuckling. "What should we eat?"

They chatted about nothing much and Everett seemed impressed when Kalv ordered a few different things off the menu.

"Are we doing a shared table thing?" Everett asked.

Kalv gave him a curious look. "Why would we do that? This is my food."

Lyra shook her head. "Order your own, Ev… They eat way more than you would expect."

"That's why you can down a whole pizza on your own," he said.

"High metabolism," she and her uncle said simultaneously.

That elicited a laugh from all of them and they ordered their meal along with drinks. She filled them in on her encounter with an unknown dragon.

"How did you not tell me any of this," her partner asked.

"You were drunk," she answered. "Uncle Kalv, were any of the caretakers exiled here when the final war ended?"

He shook his head. "Of course not, too much of a risk. So many of them were willing to work with the Shen to subjugate humankind that sending them here would give them a chance to reorganize."

"Then I have no clue who this young dragon would be unless one ran away through the portal," Lyra commented. "And why he would be targeting me."

"This is why I'm going to stick around for a bit." Kalv looked up at the waitress and smiled, thanking her for the food. "Ginna has taken the children back to Paladin in case this is some new, rising threat. She'll advise the king."

"You know where the house is, did you ride your bike?" Lyra took a bite of her hot noodles with steak and eggs.

"Yep, parked around the corner," he answered. "I'll be shadowing you from above if necessary."

"Hey, I have to draw the line." Everett held up his hand. "I know she's your family but I'm her partner. I can watch her back."

"I am honored to know you would protect my niece." Kalv inclined her head. "But if this is a caretaker move or a rogue dragon, you or your gun won't be a match for them."

"How are you going to explain a huge-ass dragon over the skies of Arizona?" Everett demanded.

Kalv laughed out loud and drew attention to their table. "Everett, how have we been here for so long and fought a war with humans none the wiser? Besides, I didn't say I'll be there twenty-four seven. I have my own leads to follow."

"And if it connects with our case?" Everett took a bite of his meal.

Kalv met his gaze "Then I'll let you both know."

They finished their meal a bit more relaxed and made small plans to keep an eye out for this unknown dragon. Knowing that her partner and her uncle had her back, both aspects of the case made her feel much better. She could see how the dragons… her dragons, could intimidate any man but somehow Everett seemed to fit, and the out of this world aspect only seemed to throw him off his game a little. *Wait till he sees the size of my uncle in his dragon nature.* The thought made her chuckle and they both looked at her curiously. Lyra feigned an innocent look even though her thoughts amused her. For now, they would enjoy lunch and then get back to the case.

That night, they sat in her truck and followed Geoff Hart as he went about his evening routine. While he ate at an exclusive restaurant, they drank bad coffee and ate a roadside quesadilla from a non-descript food cart. They watched him go to the gym and then back to an apartment in the city and not the one he shared with his wife and son.

"I wonder how many women, including Amy, have spent time in there?" Lyra commented.

"Don't want to put a black light on that bed or

any surface," Everett added. "I don't get how people live lives like that, jumping from one partner to another, sharing each other's bodies."

"Variety, I suppose." She sipped her coffee.

"I know poly couples who are an intimate couple of three," Everett said. "They share each other's lives and love hard just like anyone else. People like Geoff Hart makes a lifestyle people choose into some sycophant playground."

"My uncles Skard and Iarl have one mate, Daphne," Lyra commented. "She loves them equally and they adore her. I have never seen a love like that."

"Wow, something like that is hard to find," Everett said gently. "So, all of these uncles, all married and happy?"

"They are mated for life." Lyra took a shallow breath. "Like we all do."

"So, you mean…" The question hung in the air.

"We love hard, we never stray, there is no argue and sleep away from each other," Lyra explained. "It's all in and if we lose our mate our dragon mourns the loss for years. It's intense so I get if you want no part of it."

He took her hand. "I think I'll take my chances."

Lyra's attention turned to the apartment. "Hey, our guy is on the move."

"Where's he going in such a rush?" Everett murmured.

They watched him get into his Mercedes, and she started the car and pulled out as Geoff's car sped by. They kept on his tail while he weaved his way through traffic. The first stop was a random bench where he reached under and took a sandwich bag that was stuck there. Geoff pulled out a cell phone and answered then started to wave his arm frantically.

He put his head in his hands while his elbows were braced on his knees and just listened. He threw the phone against the sidewalk in anger and for a moment his shoulders shook like he was sobbing. Geoff regained his composure and kicked the pieces of phone in disgust. He got back in his car and drove away.

"That's interesting," Lyra murmured. "Follow him, see if he heads back to his place. I'll meet you there after I get the phone pieced. The tech guys might be able to get something."

"How are you going to…" He waved his hand and opened the dash to give her an evidence bag. "Never mind, I've seen you move. Get out of here before I lose him."

Lyra was already out of the car and jogging

across the street and took pictures of exactly where each piece of the phone was. She used the bandana in her pocket to collect the bag and the pieces of phone before placing them carefully into her own bag. There could be fingerprints as well, so she wanted to keep everything from being contaminated. She pulled her own phone from her pocket and pressed Everett's number that was always at the top, either his or Trixie's.

"Where are you?" she asked.

"He picked up a new bottle of Jack and is heading back to his place," Everett answered.

"Be in there in ten."

Lyra disconnected the call and began cutting through cross streets to head back to the apartment high rise. He hadn't gone too far, maybe five to seven minutes by car, so her long, toned legs ate up the distance easily. She scented her quarry, the unknown dragon. He was trailing her but not close, and Lyra wanted more than anything to lead him into a trap. *I'm wearing my good sneakers; I could give him a run for his money.*

But there was more at stake—right now she wasn't important. A child was missing, and it seemed his father was being blackmailed. This might have gone from a murder by a husband to a kidnapping and extortion. So, her nemesis who liked to follow her from the shadows would have to wait. She crossed one more street and then jogged up the hill to where her truck was parked. She opened the passenger door and slipped inside before putting the evidence bag in the back seat.

"Back to drinking himself into a stupor," Everett informed her. "I think someone killed his wife and kidnapped the kid."

"His financial didn't show a thing." Lyra sighed in frustration. "If we saw massive amounts of money going in, we could assume he's laundering money for the cartel through his business. But his records are squealing clean."

"He was on a private jet. Maybe he's doing more than fixing up the rich and famous with perfect smiles," Everett countered. "Columbia, Cancun, Puerto Vallarta, all high drug trafficking points."

"If he screwed over drug cartels, his life is more than forfeit," Lyra said. "God, I hope we find Bryce. They don't care if the person they kill is a child."

"You got that right," Everett said grimly.

"We should go in there and make him tell us what he knows," Lyra said angrily. "All these days have gone by and he knew what was going on with his son, we could've been helping him!"

"He can deny it, and we have no proof, unless he specifically says hey, they have my son. We are in a holding pattern," Everett pointed out. "If we get something off that phone, then we can act."

"I want to punch him in the face," Lyra muttered. "Amy is in agony for her child, and he's being feminine hygiene product."

"And that's called a douche if you're using it as an insult." He looked at his watch. "It's almost one. Let's call a relief unit here to sit on this guy and take this to crime scene techs to see what they can pull out of it."

"I hope they get a print of the case at least, give us a clue where to look," Lyra said. "My uncle will be out doing whatever he does to procure information, and I thought we'd be gone all night."

"Then don't go home, come to my place." Everett voice took on a low, husky timber.

She looked at him curiously. "You've invited me to your place all of two times."

"That's because if I took you there, we'd probably end up in bed together," Everett pointed out.

"And you want us to end up in bed together this time around?" Lyra asked.

He sighed. "Lyra, I want to do more than kiss you. This is my way of saying let's get closer."

"I'm sorry, I have no clue about men, finesse or romance in general," Lyra admitted. "Now I'm nervous."

He gave her a smile. "You can say no. It's romance, not a test."

"No, no I want to." Lyra smiled shyly. "I have much more attraction to you than I ever did to my betrothed."

"The guy who had to get the king's permission to not marry," Everett surmised. "Was he as large of a man as your uncle?"

Lyra nodded. "Not quite as tall but formidable."

"That won't give me a complex or anything." His voice was droll.

"Why should it?"

He shook his head. "Never mind, it's a man thing."

It took another thirty minutes of waiting before an unmarked unit took over watching Geoff Hart's secret apartment. She and Everett went back to the precinct to log the evidence and plead for them to put a rush on processing the cell phone. Which meant bribery, illegal by any standard of law enforcement but within those walls the only way to jump the line sometimes.

It only cost her thick cut steaks and two bottles of the good wine she had in her wine cellar. Next time it would be up to Everett to put front the bounty. As they drove to his house, Lyra's stomach clenched with excitement and nervousness. She had never gotten to this point with a man before and while she had the urges, innocence to what men wanted had caused her to seek information from YouTube videos and online blogs.

Not the best way to learn, but Trixie's version of just bang it out didn't help either.

He parked on the quiet street of Rodeo Drive where his townhouse sat connected to three more on the lot. Everett got out and jogged around to the passenger side to open the door for her. He took her hand as they walked to his home and he unlocked the door. Inside, she looked around, refamiliarizing herself with his space and taking in his scent that permeated the air. Everett wore light cologne that enhanced his male scent. She'd always liked it but now it made her inner dragon purr. Maybe it appealed to her long before but now she was really listening to her body.

He wasn't a lot for over personalizing things, like knick-knacks and pictures. There was one of him in his dress blues when he received an award and a few other framed certificates. There wouldn't be any pictures of family—she knew of the caustic relationship he had with his mother. He had an aquarium, and she walked over to look at the fish swimming around lazily in their watery home.

She turned and ran her hands down the front of her jeans. "So how do we do this?"

Everett chuckled and flipped on the TV. "Would you like some wine or beer?"

"Wine please," Lyra answered. "Libations to relax, good start."

Everett shook his head. "Take it easy, it's not a step-by-step process. It's a let it flow see where the night takes us thing."

"And if take it take us nowhere?" she prodded.

"Then I still spend time with one beautiful woman who happens to be my partner and a damn great cop," he answered.

That reply pleased her, and she took off her coat as he got glasses from his small kitchen. She sat on the dark beige sofa and looked at the news as it played across the screen.

He sat beside her and handed her a glass. "Not like the stuff you have at your place but it's good."

Lyra tasted it and let the muscadine grape flavor play across her taste buds. "It's a North Carolina wine, I like their selections."

"I should take you to Napa Valley. Your taste buds would rival their pretentious connoisseurs." Everett took a swing of his own beer.

"I'd like that. Trixie told me there is a wine

train thing, and we still have to get that planned," Lyra said.

"She wouldn't be invited," Everett told her. "This would be a you and me thing, where we spend the night in some quaint hotel and do the tourist thing."

"Why, Detective Everett Craig, I would never take you as the bed-and-breakfast antiquing type," Lyra teased.

He gave her a fake somber look. "I have layers to my complex personality."

She lifted her glass in a silent toast. "I see that. Consider me schooled."

"There is more to come," he promised huskily.

Sitting with him, her body relaxed, and instead of worrying about what would happen next, she enjoyed his company. The case wasn't far from their thoughts, but there wasn't much they could do until crime scene got them information. It was nice to just be with him and listen to him talk. Or did she? Because it seemed that she'd fallen asleep when he nudged her gently.

"Hey, Princess, let's get you to bed," Everett said gently.

"Not royalty here, just Lyra," she murmured. "I'm not sleeping."

"Sure, you're not." He kissed her temple and helped her to her feet. "Even otherworldly dragons need to sleep."

"You're going to sleep with me," she murmured and pressed a kiss against his neck.

He groaned. "If you keep that up, there will be no sleeping involved.

Sleep suddenly was very far from her mind. "Well then, show me."

That was when his lips met hers, and Everett walked them backward to the open door of his bedroom. The heat floored her. The way he kissed her heightened her senses to the feel of his body, from the way his shoulders bunched and the muscles tensed under her hands to the way he pressed her to him and cupped her hips. The new sensations exhilarated her and dared her to sample more.

"I don't know how to do any of this, will you teach me?" Lyra asked tentatively.

Everett cupped her cheeks. "It would be my pleasure. You are the most beautiful woman I have ever seen."

The way he called her beautiful, when in this world her strength made her feel like she didn't belong. Tears pricked her eyes and she was never one to cry. Even in her worst times with her father, after her mother died, no matter what she had never shed a tear. Now one man gently caressed her face and ran the pad of his thumb over her bottom lip. It felled her and caused a sweet ache in her heart.

Lyra could tell when a person was lying. It was a scent, something that came out in their sweat glands. Everett was being honest, even if she couldn't sense it, she didn't doubt he was telling the truth. By the Gods, it made something inside her heart do a tumble and excited and caused her fear at the same time. Yet she wasn't about to resist the temptation, after the kiss they shared they had to be more to experience.

She pushed him suddenly and sent him back on his perfectly made bed. Compared to the piles of blankets that she fondly called her nest, his bedroom was pristine. *I should ask him about this,* Lyra thought as she covered his body with her own and pressed her lips against his. He wrapped his hands around her waist and took control of the kiss. Much to her delight, the same sensations that curled in her belly gained in intensity. With a quick roll their positions were reversed, and Lyra was settled under his hard body. His kiss devastated her senses, and she could feel the heat of his body through his t-shirt and the hardness of his cock between her legs.

"We're hitting the point of no return," he said

huskily. "I want you — hell, I've wanted you since I met you. Say no and kick me out to the couch if you want to take it slow."

"Show me everything." Lyra reached down to pull his shirt over his head. "You arouse me."

Everett groaned. "That is the most innocent and sexist thing I ever heard."

She kissed the soft skin at his neck and licked it gently, taking him and committing it to memory.

"Your mouth on my skin is very distracting," he murmured.

Lyra looked at him. "But I wish I could show you more."

"Go with your instincts," he replied huskily.

The words ceased and were replaced with kisses that became more intimate, deeper, and filled with heat. Everett's hands moved hungrily over her body. This time it was him who kissed her neck, and the heat of his lips made Lyra shiver. She slipped away to undress, and his gaze followed her every move hungrily. She seldom wore a bra, so her breasts spilled free from her top and a husky sound escaped him.

"Show me all of you." Everett's voice was almost primal.

Lyra held her breath as she finished removing her clothes and left herself open and bare to him.

She was suddenly self-conscious and covered her breasts with her hands.

"Don't ever hide yourself from me," Everett ordered gently. "Now come here, kneel on the bed, and spread your legs."

Lyra did as she was told and watched her expression when he cupped the mound between her legs. Lyra gasped when she felt his finger slip between the lips of her sex.

"You are so damn wet already," he murmured. "My god, how did I go so long without touching you?"

Lyra leaned over to kiss him. "You should come reap the rewards."

She laughed when Everett flipped from the bed and wasted no time getting undressed. He was completely naked, and she watched each muscle of his body climbed into the bed to cover her body. Just looking at him made Lyra lick her lips in anticipation. Everett kissed his way from her torso to the apex of her thighs. She held her breath when his lips kissed the mound. Lyra moaned when he ran his tongue up the slit of her pussy. While she didn't understand the sensation, she wanted more.

His guttural groan of approval filled the room, and he pulled her thighs to him. Lyra closed her eyes and arched her head into the pillows while Everett devoured her in such an intimate way. She cried out in pleasure.

"Do you like how that feels?" He lifted his head.

"Yes," she answered. "What else is there?"

"Trust me," he said with a smile and settled to where he was once more.

Everett spread the tender lips of her sex to suck and tease her clit. By the gods, the sensations was unlike anything she ever knew. Lyra trembled and her hips raised in earnest, seeking more of the intimate action from his mouth. Was this what she had missed all her life? Was this how it always was?

His tongue penetrated her, and she thought she would almost die from the intense feelings. Lyra called his name, uncertain of what was building inside her. Yet she pleaded for more as her body became flush with desire.

Everett stopped and covered her body. "Baby, those noises are killing me. I want to fuck you right now."

"Then do it," Lyra said eagerly.

"Oh honey," he kissed her. "I need to make you ready."

He gripped her cheek with one hand and kissed her hard, spearing his tongue in her mouth until she whimpered, and she was lost all over again. *Yes,* she thought, loving his primal, rough touch as he ran his hands all over her body. Impatience filled her—she didn't want slow or gentle, she was ready to experience it all. Lyra wanted Everett to make her body his. He wrenched his mouth away from hers, leaving her gasping once more.

Everett's lips did delicious things to her while he kissed his way back down her body. After wrapping his arms around her thick thigh to anchor her to him, he teased and tasted her sensitive flesh causing her to cry out and writhe under his onslaught. *Dear lord.* She was going to melt into the bed from the heat of his mouth. He didn't let go or stop until she came hard under his pleasurable assault and she was left gasping.

"What... was... that?" The words were punctuated by each breath.

"That was an orgasm baby, I love how you come for me." His voice was gravelly with desire.

"Can we do it again?" she gasped in excitement while ecstasy still coursed through her body.

"How about this," he murmured and lay next to her.

First, he licked and sucked at her aching nipples until he sucked them into his mouth. Lyra closed her eyes, enjoying this new heat. Everett replaced his mouth with his fingers at her pussy and pressed them deep inside her. She could feel his eyes on her watching the build-up and causing to her writhe in his arms and against his finger. He found that secret place within her sex that drove her wild, and Lyra screamed in surprise and elation. She arched her head into the pillow as his pace increased. Somehow the movements of his hand not only filled her sex, but the upward motion grazed her clit heightening the sensations.

Everett's actions sent her careening into a firestorm of bliss. Lyra was drowning in pleasure. She was unable to hold back the soft wail that left her lips. Her release tore through her, and she coated his fingers with her essence.

"Bless it, oh that was incredible." Lyra tried to catch her breath.

"I could watch you all day," Everett's voice was low. "I need to be inside you."

She spread her legs eagerly. "Please."

He positioned himself kneeling between her legs and his breath hissed out looking at her wet sex. She reached out to stroke his cock, loving the feel of the smooth head. Lyra gasped as his rod throbbed in her grasp. Everett ran the tip of his rod against her pussy coating the head with her juices. He slipped into her slowly allowing her to get accustomed to the penetration.

"All of it," she demanded.

Everett pressed himself inside her with one deep, hard thrust that caused them both to cry out, her because of the sharp pain and him at the gratification of their union. He waited, and she heard his harsh breathing and his body trembled as he strived for control. She lifted her hips, testing the sensation and liking the feel of his cock inside her. Everett kissed her as he began to move, slowly at first so she could learn the first rhythm of two bodies mating.

Their rhythm increased. All the while he kissed her, teased her nipples with his lips and made her feel like she was treasured and powerful all at once. She could feel his cock thicken within her as the pace caused the band to tighten within her. Everett thrust into her, and Lyra lifted her hips, spreading her legs wider, meeting his hard thrusts and ferocious need with her own. He bent his head and sucked one pert tip deeply into his mouth, causing her to arch beneath him.

"More!" The voice sounded like hers, but it was filled with sexual demand.

"Oh fuck, Lyra, yes baby, come for me," his voice was a primal growl.

She felt the walls of her pussy clench around his rod before she arched as the heat coursed over in waves. Her body tensed while she came, and it was like a meteor shower over the falls of Paladin. Everett was far from done with her. He flipped her over until she was on her hands and knees.

He kissed her lower back and she arched. "You'll like this, I promise baby."

Lyra could feel the head of his manhood as he probed her sex from the new position. She moaned wantonly as he slid into her from behind. Everett made her tremble when he reached around her thighs to rub her clit. It felt so good, she couldn't help but undulate against his length.

Her movements made him groan. "Yeah, you like that don't you, take more of my cock, baby."

Everett thrust deep and she cried out, the sound muffled in the pillow. Lyra was reeling from the strength of her desire to feel him completely immersed in her pussy even though this was her first time. Her dragon purred within her mind—mating, sexuality it all connected them, and her second nature was pleased with her choice of a mate and the sensations coursing through her body.

He withdrew, and she felt him glide against the walls of her sex before he plunged again. Lyra arched her back as Everett grabbed her hips and increased his pace, soon he was pounding into her. The sound of their bodies meeting was a wet, delicious and decadent, and she cried out.

"Jesus, I can't hold back," Everett said through gritted teeth. "Oh shit, I'm going to come so deep inside you."

"Do it," Lyra moaned. "Let me feel it, fill me."

She felt his thrusts deepen, each one more pleasurable than the last. He pumped into her feverishly. Lyra lost herself in the moment, the mating between them was fierce and that stoked the dragon fire inside her.

When Lyra's orgasm took hold, it rocked her body, and it was like soaring into the sky with her wings spread to the stars. Her moans of completion were muffled against the pillows. Her sex clenched in delight as his low guttural cry followed hers. She reveled in the feeling of his seed filling her core, a new contentment that made her dragon purr and rub sensually against the boundaries of her mind that separated them. Everett's body settled against hers, and he pressed soft kisses on her shoulder and neck making her smile.

"Now that was worth waiting for," she murmured in contentment.

"That's what a man loves to hear." Everett's voice was husky. "This won't change a thing as partners, except now I might be more protective of you."

"We shall protect each other, how is that?" Lyra turned to face him when he finally moved.

He brushed her thick hair away from her face and kissed her lips. "Deal."

She closed her eyes. Sleep was easy in coming and it felt amazing with his arms wrapped around her waist. Lyra would see what the new day brought. She felt more like a woman and wondered if this was the beginning of what her family had. Something that was more than friendship, after three years of working together, having it as a solid foundation was a good start.

Chapter Seven

The evidence techs managed to get some information on the broken cellphone forty-eight hours later. No fingerprints, but the tech put it back together enough to get a number and a text. The number ended up being to a burner phone that had been turned off. *Probably destroyed,* she thought grimly. But the intent of the message was clear: someone had Bryce. She and Everett agreed it was probably best not to drag Geoff Hart back in but to put him off his game.

He wasn't going to work, in fact it seemed he spent the entire weekend in his apartment drinking. While the missing person's unit traced down leads from the Amber alert that came into the tip line, he was home drowning his sorrows. That pissed Lyra off. Only the Gods knew what Bryce was dealing with and every day that passed meant he could be slipping further and further away.

It was eight a.m. when they banged on his front door, and after the night he probably had

Lyra was sure that their presence would not be welcomed. She was proven correct when the door was flung open and Geoff stood before them disheveled with red-rimmed eyes. His appearance had taken a turn for the worse.

His shirt hung out of his pants and there was a stain on the front of his pale green button-up shirt. His hair was not combed, he had more than a five o'clock shadow and the stench of stale whiskey and not bathed. Lyra wrinkled her nose. The stench coming from the apartment wasn't much better. She flicked her eyes behind him to see the old food cartons and beer bottles on every surface, plus whiskey bottles everywhere.

"What the fuck do you two want, my lawyer isn't here," Geoff snarled.

"Good morning, Mr. Hart. You look well," Lyra said politely.

Everett pushed past him the apartment. "My, my, some kind of party went on in here."

"I'll have your badges as soon as I call my lawyer…" Geoff snapped out.

Everett cut him off. "Stop the bullshit. We know someone is holding your son and you are up a fucking creek without a paddle."

Lyra spied something in the midst of the chaos on the coffee table. She strode forward quickly and used her little finger to pick up the small caliber gun. Beside it was a hastily written note.

"You were going to kill yourself without knowing if your son was safe?" Lyra's tone was deadly because she wanted to kill him herself at that moment.

Geoff's shoulders sagged. "It was the only way I could think of to save him."

"How about telling the police investigating your wife's murder and let them get a jump on it." Everett's voice was angry. "All this time you knew, and we were chasing down leads and following your dumb ass."

"Tell us what's going on and maybe we can bring your son home safe," Lyra said in a low tone.

He met her eyes with an agonized gaze. "Okay… okay."

They watched him silently as he walked over and sat down heavily in the first chair he came to. His whole body slumped in defeat and he put his head in his hands again.

"You know about the couples swapping," he said in a monotone. "But… I work for some shady people sometimes. Even criminals want good teeth too. One of my clients is Javier Cortez and his family."

"The Javier Cortex?" Everett asked incredulously.

"Clue me in?" Lyra asked.

"Shit." Everett began to pace. "He is one of the biggest lieutenants in the Pisano cartel. You never had to cross his path. I have when I worked in the drug unit. The man has never had a charge stick on him, and he has a whole lot of bodies to his name. He is a bad man."

Lyra looked at Geoff. "Did you take his money or his drugs?"

"Worse. His daughter," Geoff answered. "She's twenty-four and on my cock from the first time we met. Have you ever had a connection that was so instantaneous that you are addicted to each other from the very beginning?"

Lyra glanced at Everett and looked away. "I wouldn't know."

"Trust me, it was like being dipped in lava. This girl had me wrapped around her finger and I didn't notice how fucking insane she was." Geoff laughed. "Maybe the clue was how she and her father talked to each other. One minute they're screaming and she's firing shots at his head. The next he's buying her a lion cup because she wanted one."

"Uhhhh, yeah, that would be a big warning sign," Lyra said.

"Her father actually warned me about her." Geoff laughed again. "Would you believe, I'm laundering the man's money and he's more worried about telling me his kid is a psycho."

"So, you broke up and now he's taken your kid to get back at you?" Everett asked.

"Not him… her!" Geoff cried out.

"So, the text, you know what I want?" Lyra prodded.

"She wants me to grab her father's cash and meet her, then me, her, and Bryce would live happily ever after somewhere." Geoff shook his head. "Yeah, take her dad's money then he kills me while I'm trying to convince her to give me my son." He looked up at them. "I know I'm going to jail, the money laundering, I have records and hell, maybe turning witness against him would get me a new life somewhere. But I need to bring Bryce home, at least give Amy that peace. I know you think I'm a bastard, I really am, but not to the point of seeing my son hurt for my mistakes."

"Where would she go, do you have any idea?" Lyra was wondering if she could find the place by flying above to take in the lay of the land.

"Her father has no clue. He's trying to find her himself. This puts his operation in jeopardy, and he begged me to keep it from the police. He even offered me two million to keep it quiet,"

Geoff explained. "You guys keep coming around and we're having no luck. Rita learned how to hide from the best. At this point, the more erratic she gets the more I worry about Bryce."

Everett turned away and got on the phone while Lyra kept her attention on Geoff, hoping to glean more information. "You said her father, but what about you? You were sleeping with Rita. She thinks she loves you and you love her. Where would she go? Where did you hide from Monica and her father?"

"I've gone through the list: hotels, private houses, condos," Geoff said. "She's gone ghost. She calls or emails to tell me where to get a cell phone. Then she says, are you ready to come home? I tell her I can't leave because the police are still investigating my wife's murder. I told her I'm trying to protect her." He shook his head. "Maybe she believes me, maybe not, but she's getting impatient. She might have a few guys working for her to scoop me up when she thinks the coast is clear."

"So, she killed Monica," Lyra concluded.

Geoff nodded. "She admitted it, pure nicotine to the bloodstream. Her father taught her well."

Everett came back from the call. "I updated the lieutenant and we're getting a team over here to trace the phone line."

Lyra's mind was working. "I have a better idea—we close the case. Put it all over the news that we are arresting Geoff for murder and he's on the run."

"She'll try to snatch him to save the man she loves and complete her family, and we can follow them to Bryce," Everett mused. "This could work, but brass will have to sign off on it."

Geoff looked from her to Everett. "What about my deal? I want witness protection if I'm going to turn over my records on Javier."

"One thing at a time," Everett said. "Federal will want to take point on that part. Right now, we want to get your son home safe."

Geoff sighed. "I get that… shit. I fucked up my life and my wife is dead because of it."

"Spare me the self-pity. You screwed up Amy's life as well with all you've put her through, which is the exact same thing Rita Cortez is doing to you right now," Lyra snapped.

Geoff looked at her. "You don't like me, do you?"

"I don't have to like you, just save your son's life and yours," she answered.

"Witness protection is no place to raise a child. I'll be a target till the day I die," he surmised. "Can we get my lawyer here so I can sign over parental rights to Amy and David? It's best for Bryce to never know this part of my life."

Lyra nodded. "That can be arranged."

He was right, she really didn't like him in the least. His greed and lust cost one woman her life and almost ruined other people's lives. She never understood how people could put themselves above people they loved. It took a few hours to get everything set up, including informing the FBI who they had and what was going on.

They would want their pound of flesh and if it meant they got on the news for bringing down a drug lord, well, the FBI was all over that like white on rice. Of course, that meant this first operation would have some of their agents on standby to swoop Geoff away when they finally got Bryce safe. He at least knew that he was a walking dead man even under federal protection. But then she had to wonder about his motivation.

Was this to help his son or another way to selfishly live his life with no reminders of his past? In the end, Lyra didn't care. Amy seemed like a genuinely good mother. She still hadn't met David to get an impression of him. Her hope was that this would be a blimp in Bryce's life and the rest would be filled with happy memories. She knew how it was to grow up unhappy, she didn't want that for any child.

After some dispute, it was agreed that to cut

down on Rita getting suspicious because the FBI was greedy to get info on Javier they would leave one plain clothes unit outside along with the Tucson police department's undercover unit. They wanted to limit too many people going in and out as well, so until they broke the news the next afternoon, it was a sit and wait. That didn't mean they could leave him completely alone in case he decided to get cold feet and run. Since it was Lyra and Everett who went in, they would be babysitting Geoff inside his apartment.

She wrinkled her nose in disgust, looking around. "If I have to sit in this place overnight, something has to be done about the junk and the smell."

Geoff waved his hand around. "Have at it. Mi casa es su casa."

Lyra snorted. "Trust me when I say I will not be cleaning up after you or anyone. How about you go shower then come do that yourself?"

He looked at Everett. "She does not have a nice disposition. Slamming body but the personality of broken shards of glass."

"How about I turn you to ash." Lyra stepped forward.

Everett held her back. "Geoff go make yourself presentable and come clean your shit up."

Geoff chuckled as he walked away. "What was she going to do, light me on fire?"

"I would enjoy hearing the fat sizzle off his bones," Lyra muttered.

Everett pressed his hand against his stomach. "The mental image just made my stomach roll. Don't let him rile you up, he's not worth it."

Lyra dusted off a lone chair and sat down. "I am going to be thrilled to see him gone after we get Bryce back. The feds should dump him in a well for witness protection."

"I think they have to give him a home and food, you know, life essentials." Everett laughed, walked behind her, and put his large hands on her shoulders.

"Trolls live in wells and under bridges just fine." She rolled her neck as he started to rub her tight muscles. "I'm going to follow from above, you get that, right?"

"Yeah, I know, but in daylight that won't be easy."

"We have our ways." Lyra smiled up at him. "But I'll need my clothes satchel so I can store my cell, gun, and clothes."

"After the news posts the report we're going to have to be on him," Everett said. "He's supposed to go to that express motel and then reach out to Rita."

"I can get Uncle Kalv to bring what I need," Lyra said. "He looks like a biker, anyway. He'll fit in with the place."

"Tell him to be inconspicuous." Everett sighed. "I don't need lieutenant asking why we know bikers; the lies are going to start piling up fast if we aren't careful."

Lyra gave him a cool look and her tone took a hint of frost. "Give us some credit. Long before you even knew about my second nature, my people were policing this world in their own way. You wouldn't have known a thing without me revealing myself to you."

"And don't you think somewhere in there your people should've trusted someone?" he shot back.

"Many people aided in the final war, including an LAPD police officer who is now married to my Uncle Gerard," Lyra shot back. "I get it, you like honesty above all things because your mother mentally screwed you up. But while I may be new to the earth realm, I do know that your people in authority tend to destroy what they don't understand."

An angry fire burned her chest as she spoke. "They kiss babies and rape the lands of their own planet. There shouldn't be a term like 'third world countries,' it's all one place, yet millions live in poverty while the rich live in their towers and look down at everyone else. What do you think they'd do if they knew about Paladin, dragons, and me?"

"I get all you're saying, I just don't like not being an up and up one hundred percent honest cop," Everett retorted.

Lyra stood and walked toward the door. "Then by all means don't let me or my kind soil your very high personal standards."

"Where are you going?" Everett asked impatiently.

"I'll wait in the car. The air is stale enough in here as is," she called over her shoulder.

"Fuck!"

She heard the harsh word escape his lips and then the sound of something being knocked off the cluttered coffee table. Lyra walked out into the evening and unlocked her truck before climbing behind the steering wheel. What she wouldn't be doing was to make any excuses for her second nature or her people who had saved the earth realm more times than the archives of Paladin could count. Humans were not only destructive to their home but to themselves.

She had let him in, but it seemed Everett wanted to know the truth as long as he could restrict it or tie it in a tidy, neat box so it suited his own life. She wasn't about to live in a mental cage just because the sex was good. It was amazing but that wasn't the point. *Everett better get over himself,* she thought as she stared sourly at the apartment building. She was a damn good cop, lover, and she lived with honor. Her dragon was part of her and one that carried with pride. If that was a problem for him then they were doomed before they really even began.

The news cast went off without a hitch, and Geoff's face was plastered all over the television. He waited a few hours before he left for the no tell motel, and they were right on his heels. Only a few clipped words were spoken between them, and the cab of the truck was thick with the tense air between them as they followed Geoff in his Mercedes from a discreet distance.

"Is your uncle bringing your satchel?" Everett asked.

"He is, and he knows to keep out of sight." Lyra's tone was brisk.

"We going to talk about this?" He changed lanes to keep the car in sight.

"We're working. Our personal issues aren't involved right now," she replied. "When Rita takes him, I'll get out of sight and shift to follow."

"I'll keep watch…"

"No," she cut him off. "I'll be fine. It's obvious me that my people are ugly to you."

"I never said that, I don't think that at all," he protested.

"That's what I took from the entire conversation," she said. "My second nature is my own and not for your eyes."

Everett cursed under his breath but let the conversation drop. Maybe he sensed her stubbornness or maybe what she said was the truth. Her dragon yowled and mourned their distance, the connection between Everett and herself seemed blurred. But they couldn't focus on that now. After a thirty- minute drive outside of Tucson, Geoff pulled into the motel and hurried in to pay for the room while they watched from the far side of the lot. The FBI were in a beat-up old truck and on the opposite side while Geoff took the fifth room in on the bottom floor.

It was a waiting game now. Would Rita show up with Bryce in her arms? Would it be over without her having to take her second nature? This was the worst part, the anticipation of the chase or the final showdown. She hoped the FBI could keep their weapons holstered in the event Rita did show up or didn't jump the gun to arrest her men. For sure Bryce would be doomed if that happened, everything was so up in the air. Her uncle rode in on his classic bike and parked on the opposite side where the FBI couldn't see his bike.

"Hey, youngling." He threw the pack at Everett's open window. "That what you need?"

"That's it, Uncle Kalv." Lyra's smile was stiff.

His gaze went from her to Everett. "Y'all okay? It's a swamp soup of tension between you two."

"All fine here." Everett's voice was glum.

"Like Aunt Ginna says, peachy keen," Lyra answered.

"Your Aunt Ginna also said two pole cats can't climb a greased pole," Kalv replied. "I think I'm on to something with our other problem. I'll let you both know."

"What a euphemism," Everett murmured. "Let me guess, she is Texan."

Kalv nodded happily. "Exactly."

"Just call me, Uncle Kalv, knowing that is not involved with our case takes out the human factor. It's about me and besides, Everett wants no part of our deception of humanity," Lyra answered.

Everett gave her a sharp look and she stared him down.

Kalv whistled. "Yeah, peachy keen. Remember, two pole cats."

"What the heck does that pole cat thing mean?" Everett asked as Kalv roared away on the bike.

"Ginna is from earth, you tell me," Lyra replied coolly.

"Christ, you're making this more than it actually was," Everett said in exasperation.

"Are we working a case?" Lyra asked. "Because if we are, our personal issues need not be discussed at this time."

"Fine, but this isn't over," Everett said between gritted teeth.

She looked out the window of the truck. "Maybe it is before it even started."

Her somber words caused her heart to ache and from the shocked, hurt look on Everett's face, he understood what she meant as well. Knowing her and her second nature, the life she had to keep a secret, there would always be some level of dishonesty. The simple truth was if he couldn't deal with that fact, he may not be the right mate for her. Her dragon yowled within her mind, unhappy with the thoughts swirling about in her head.

A dark sedan pulled into the motel parking lot off the highway and parked rather haphazardly in front of the door where Geoff was now holed up. Two men jumped out, both wearing sunglasses and dressed like the typical bad guy, dark pants and t-shirts with a gold chain around their necks. They stood outside the car, assessing the area and looking for anyone. Both she and Everett went low in the cab in the truck so they would be unseen.

"Hold, do nothing. Let them take him and lead us to the baby," Everett said lowly into the walkie they were using to keep in contact with their FBI backup.

A staticky reply to confirm came back over the radio. Lyra waited until they were inside to make her move. She grabbed her satchel from the backseat.

"That line of trees to the left is where I'm going. I'll call you and you bring in the cavalry when I know where Bryce is."

"I'll tell them you followed the car using our dirt bike or something," Everett replied.

"That's fine."

Lyra heard the crispness in her tone before she slipped from the cab of the truck. She made a mad dash behind the little hotel to the small outcropping of trees and quickly took her clothes off and shoved them along with her sidearm into the dragon satchel. It was almost an eager change as she gave herself over to her second nature, a way to get out of her skin since the human part of her was in the midst of strife with her partner slash lover. Compared to the men of Paladin when they shifted, she was smaller. It didn't mean she was any less formidable, and she took to the skies. The sun refracted off her dark red scales and made her invisible as she glided through the air. It was just as the sedan pulled out from the motel, kicking up the gravel when it left the pavement.

Lyra gave one large flap of her leathery wings and glided. The feeling of the wind currents changing and shifting across her scales was one of the great pleasures that almost wiped her issues with Everett from her mind. The car Geoff drove left whatever traffic there was and made a turn on a secondary road, that seemed more dirt that asphalt and the time droned by.

When the sign for Flagstaff came up, she estimated she had been in the sky for a little more than three hours and that meant the drive for Everett and the FBI boys would be just as long. Lyra wasn't dumb, she would wait for back up but if she got an inkling Bryce was in danger that plan was going out the window fast.

Finally, about thirty minutes after the Flagstaff sign, the sedan pulled next to a small Pueblo house in an area where the indigenous people still lived. The car pulled up to one structure that was set off around thirty feet from the main area of the town.

The roof was flat, and beams stuck out from the stone, making a small awning covered with vines that ran from the wood down the trellis. There was a small courtyard with a fountain in the center of the Spanish tile with more flowers and plants one wouldn't expect to bloom in the middle of the dessert. Many people thought only cactus could grow in these areas. But as long as the roots were deep enough to find water, or the landscape was cared for, many things grew in the desert eutopia.

She watched as the men got out of the car. They dragged Geoff from the passenger seat. *Jackpot,* Lyra thought triumphantly and watched them take him inside. She looked for somewhere she could shift easily and make it back to the pueblo house. Without trees to hide her, the next best bet was an outcropping of rocks.

She found one close enough that she could walk back to the small house and use a smaller set of rocks for cover till her re-enforcements arrived. Her dragon gave a disappointed yowl as she took control of her skin and human form and dressed quickly. From her new vantage point, Lyra took her cell from her pocket and pressed the familiar icon to Everett's number.

"You okay?" Everett asked in lieu of hello. "It's been hours, I started to worry."

"Perfect," she said smoothly. "They're in a pueblo house outside the Box Canyon Ruins. She has a cozy little love den between Flagstaff and the ruins set off from everyone else."

"That's a few hours out, do you have cover until we can get there?"

"Yes, and I have water in my pack and a few protein bars," she answered. "Get the FBI and hit the road, I'll be waiting."

"Don't do anything until we get there," Everett ordered.

"If this goes south and I think Bryce is in danger, I'm going in for him," Lyra said honestly. "You don't like lies so I figured I'd tell you upfront."

"Me and you are going to hash this out," Everett promised. "You may be a dragon princess and shit, but I will be damned if I don't get my say then fuck the hell out of you after. Be there as quick as we can."

With that he hung up, and she looked at the phone for a moment and a slow smile spread across her face. *Who knew I liked a dominant man?* Apparently, she did since his words gave her a sudden burst of desire. Lyra settled into the wait, looking at the time on her phone and estimating they should be there by at least seven that evening. Lyra trained her eyes and opened her senses as she stared at the house. If anything happened, she was ready to react.

Chapter Eight

The sun was a beautiful burnt orange that settled behind the rocks that Arizona was known for. Through time, wind and rain had formed the monolithic pieces, carved by the gods. Each stone was a new type of art that could take your breath away with the beauty. Lyra never got tired of the scenes, the way the landscape changed in earth realm. She saw why her mother loved it so, why the woman she had almost forgotten wanted to come back against her father's wishes. Lyra looked at the time, wishing Everett and their people and the FBI would hurry the hell up.

That's when the first cry came to her ears, low, a baby and then another. Lyra moved to where she could see better and focused on the courtyard. Geoff rushed out, holding the baby in his arms. Bryce was crying and Geoff held the baby's head to his shoulder. The two guards came out, one had a gun trained on the man and baby. That image sent anger coursing through Lyra's veins, especially when the woman walked out casually and didn't say a word to stop them.

She was beautiful, dark long hair and olive skin that seem to catch the last rays of the sun. Her curves were to die for, and her tall heels only seemed to accentuate her body. Lyra picked up their conversation easily as she moved closer in case she needed to act. From her position she started to strip knowing that if things went bad, the dragon would be needed more than a woman with a gun. She picked up her clothes and shoved them into the pack to take with her.

"Let me go," Geoff implored. "Let me take him home and you can do anything you want with me."

"I want the baby too!" Rita stomped her foot. "A baby, and I still look like this plus the man I love."

"Shit, he does pick conceited women," Lyra murmured, thinking about Monica and all the cosmetic surgery she had done. If they were doing it for themselves great, but if this was a requirement for his affection, then it was idiotic.

"Rita, you don't love me," Geoff said firmly. "You like to think so because your father said no."

"I don't care what that man thinks," Rita denied.

"Yeah, but yet you're fucking someone just like him… me." Geoff sneered. "In essence, you're doing your father just go get back at him."

Rita reached out her arms to take the baby from Geoff. It was a struggle, and it wasn't until her men made him give her Bryce that he let his son go.

"You know, Geoff, your mouth was always good for so many things except keeping your cool." Rita bounced the baby and crooned to him gently. "But I think you're right. I have my son, I can find a mouth anywhere. Kill him."

"No!" Geoff cried out.

Rita's man aimed the gun, and she heard the shot as her dragon took form quickly. When she flew up from behind the rocks, it was with a roar and she trained her attention on the men in the courtyard. They screamed and fired wildly. One bullet grazed her scales, and she dropped the pack from her claws behind the wall as she landed just outside the courtyard. The wall crumbled, brick and clay went to dust under her feet. While it would have been satisfying to char them all, there would be no way to explain that.

With a swipe of her tail she knocked them into the far side of the brick structure. Watching them fall and lay motionless gave her infinite satisfaction. She heard Rita scream and saw her from the window before the woman rushed deeper into the home. Lyra took control of her body again. Her dragon voiced its disapproval in her mind they didn't die in flames from her breath. She dressed in the fastest time possible before she took her gun and made her way to the back door.

"Rita Cortez, this is the Tucson Police, I need you to come on out," Lyra called.

"There's a monster out there, El diablo himself!" Rita cried out. "He's come to take my soul."

Lyra heard the cars before she saw them—the sound of wheels meeting gravel as they turned off the road.

"There is no one out here," Lyra called back. "I think your father's rivals attacked the house."

Everett and the FBI as well as two plain clothed officers climbed over the wall. "We've got four in front."

She pointed at Geoff. "Check him for vitals."

"Damn it, he was the best source for Cortez's operation," one of the FBI men raged. "This was a bad idea, why didn't you stop them?"

Lyra gave him an incredulous look. "One woman, and you people took your time getting here. You wanted me to go in alone? Let me be clear, he means nothing to me. The child is my concern, not some narcissistic asshole who slept with the wrong woman."

The second agent checked on Geoff. "Looks like he got grazed and one in the shoulder. I'll call for an ambulance."

"She's inside with the baby. She thinks the devil came for her," Lyra said loudly. "A monster, but I think it was Cortez's rivals."

"Looks like they did a number on her wall," Everett commented looking at Lyra.

"Could be anyone," the agent said.

"Rita, let me come in and help you," Lyra said gently. "No one wants to hurt you and the baby is crying."

"Yes, come in… only you!" Rita called back frantically.

"Be careful, if she's as crazy as they say..." Everett let his words fall away.

Lyra put her gun in the back of her jeans. "Oh, she is, trust me. She took the baby and told them to shoot Geoff."

She stepped inside the simply furnished pueblo house. The strange thing was all the rose petals on the ground and the candles and wine that sat in an ornate silver bowl. Rita was ready for romance, but Geoff had only wanted his son. At least Lyra could commend him on that part. She sat on the chair, juggling the baby on her lap.

Bryce seemed well fed and happy as he looked around. Rita managed to soothe him with graham cracker cookies, and he sat chewing one.

"You look good as a mother," Lyra said gently. She warily stepped closer, ready for any move that Rita may make that could put her life in jeopardy.

Rita smiled. "I think so, much better than the one he had. She was barely watching him, didn't even put on his floaties in case he fell into the water."

"I think they had just got there," Lyra said. "Everyone said Monica loved Bryce."

"His name is Noel," Rita said. "Like the Christmas song."

Lyra smiled. "I like it."

Rita sighed. "I have to give him to you, don't I?"

"Yes, you do." Lyra didn't see the point of lying. "He has to go to his real mother, and I want to get you help."

Fat tears fell down her cheeks and Lyra felt sorry for the young woman as she spoke. "I just wanted a regular family, not in a caged compound with guns and men I don't know coming in and out. Do you know two of my father's deputies raped me at seventeen? He killed them, yes, but he told me to be a strong girl and move on. Who moves on from that with the same type of people walking around? I guess now I will be free of it all."

"In a way, yes," Lyra answered. "Let me take him, Rita. You'll have a life yet after all this, you are young."

"You think so?" Rita said hopefully. She wiped her eyes and smeared her mascara.

"I do, far away from your father and everything you hate," Lyra answered. "Everyone should have the life they want. You'll get yours if you really want to make a difference."

Rita smiled. "Thank you."

She allowed Lyra to take Bryce and call Everett in to arrest her. In the end, Geoff was in the hospital and the FBI was happy they still had their information cash cow. Lyra was able to take Bryce home that night, to the familiar face of his real mother Amy. He squealed and held out his hands to her eagerly, excited to see a familiar face. and she held him and kissed his chubby cheeks as her tears flowed. They finally met David, her husband who seemed just as relieved as his wife to have Bryce home.

"Thank you," he said gratefully. "We can put all this behind us."

"What will you do now?" Lyra asked.

Amy looked up at her husband. "We're

moving to Seattle; his job wants him to take a lead position there. We can start over and put this behind us."

"Won't you miss the sun," Everett teased.

David smiled sadly. "I don't think so. I put my wife through some shit for some crazy urge to see what was out there. It was never worth her or our love. I plan to make the sunshine for her wherever we are."

Lyra felt a sweet ache in her heart at his words. "You do that, Amy can reach me. I can travel with my gun."

They all laughed at that, but in the back of her mind, Lyra was dead serious. After the goodbyes and the door of the apartment closed, it was her and Everett, alone.

"We need to talk," Everett said as they walked back to the truck.

"Not right now. We need to get the write ups done and close this case, send it to the DA, and then I'm going to home to eat and drink a bottle of wine," Lyra said tiredly.

"I don't think we should let this fester," he pushed.

"Probably not, but I said I don't want to talk right now, and I meant it." She pivoted on her heels and faced him. "This whole thing has been exhausting, including the argument and feeling like I'm not up to your standards. So, my plan is work, food, and wine."

"Maybe you're right, decisions should be made with clear heads." Everett strode toward the elevator.

That didn't sound like it boded well for a blooming relationship and inside she felt a pang of an ache in her chest. Still, now wasn't the right time to discuss where they were going. Lyra could sense his disapproval, but then her dragon was none too happy either.

One would think that she would get one night of peace. After following Geoff and the whole arrest she was exhausted and hungry. So much so that while they sat on the desk, she ordered the entire squad pizza, wings, and fries. She ate her fill and the cola she drank gave her some extra energy. But by midnight Lyra actually left the precinct. She was over the day and it was her day off, so her plan was to sleep in. Everett opted to take a cab home; they shared a car so frequently he rarely drove his. When they finally discussed a path the couple might take, if they didn't share each other's views then he could be driving himself.

Lyra was already wondering if she should transfer to Vice or special crimes. The couples on every show she ever watched when she got to the earth realm that made her want to join the ranks of police officers had burned hot and bright and then fizzled into cold, tense words and interactions. All the while they secretly still loved each other and craved the passion. She couldn't do that and work side by side with him each day. So, if they broke up, Lyra would move to another precinct because she and her dragon would long for him.

As she drove home, her mind was everywhere and nowhere all at once. The light went green, and she pulled out into the intersection and that was when the car hit the broadside of her truck and spun it around. The impact knocked the wind from her lungs and as the glass shattered and sprayed everywhere, she banged her head against the wheel and then the door.

Finally, there was silence and she tried to get her bearings. Her head hurt and the crash had silenced her dragon. Pain bloomed from her side and radiated up her left arm. Lyra struggled to get herself free the best she could with the use of one hand. She stumbled out of the truck and a wave of dizziness assaulted her senses and almost drove her to the ground.

"Hello, princess, time to die."

The voice came from behind her, and she struggled to her feet knowing that if she didn't defend herself, she would be dead. Her uncle was nowhere around nor Everett. She was alone and had to fight for her life. No one was around, businesses were closed for the night and the streets were deserted. Lyra stumbled down the closest alley, with her arm against her chest.

She wasn't too far from the precinct, if she could make it back… her assailant shoved her, and she pitched forward to the ground. *Fight!* Her mind screamed the word, but the head wound meant she couldn't connect with her second nature. She rolled to the side and brought her long legs up for a kick that connected to her attacker's torso. The blow caught him on the chin, and she heard the sword he held scrape against the asphalt.

"Who the hell are you?" Lyra asked angrily. "Why are you hunting me?"

Instead of words, he swung his sword at her center, and she dodged his moves with nothing to defend herself. Keeping out of the way of the blade was the only option. When she saw an opening at his right side, Lyra kidney punched him and dashed back out of the way of his weapon. He kicked and connected with her left side that had been injured. Pain sent her to her knees, and it was then that Lyra knew it was the end. She could hardly breathe, let alone get up at this point. She closed her eyes and readied herself to meet her ancestors at the table of her forefathers. Would the guardians greet her and take her to Odin himself to be judged? Would she be worthy as only half dragon?

"This is for the honor of the Hamon house." Her attacker pushed the hoodie away to reveal the man she chased in the park. "For your father and the dishonor, you have shown him and brought to his name."

He raised the long sword, and she noted the hilt held the crest of her father. All of this was because of her father—it seemed fitting, really. Hamon had caused his wife, her mother's death, and he would be the man behind hers. She closed her eyes, waiting for the metal to meet her flesh. Instead she heard a sharp clang as two weapons met. She opened her eyes and looked up to see the head of the palace guard, her ex, Dael. His own sword held the final strike to take her life and he looked down at her.

"Princess," Dael said formally. "May I offer my services?"

With a deft move, he disarmed her assailant and had him against the wall with a sword to his neck.

"How did you… when?" Lyra struggled to her feet.

"I heard the guards of Hamon talking about how he raged after you brought us to face the king," Dael answered. "I learned of his plan to kill you and came to offer my service. A peace offering against all I have done."

She opened her mouth to ask more questions, but the sound of a Harley cut off her words. Expecting to see her Uncle Kalv, she was even more surprised when it was not only him who climbed off the wide seat but Everett as well. Both rushed up, and Everett pulled her into his arms.

"Are you okay?" Everett murmured into her hair.

"Not particularly. I think I broke my arm and a few ribs," she gasped out in pain. "Please let go."

"Shit! We need to get you to a hospital." Everett pulled out his phone.

"No, I'll heal at home," she said. "How did you find me?"

"Someone called in an accident when I was turning into your place," Everett explained. "They called your license plate. I pounded on your door for your Uncle and he made me ride bitch on his bike."

"Ah," she said.

Kalv's large hand replaced Dael's sword at her attacker's throat. "Tell me why I shouldn't kill you for the Princess?"

"He should stand before the king with his master, Hamon," Dael said. "I learned of the plot and have been watching him since then. I was unable to stop the automobile's impact."

"You saved her life, the king will reward you for this," Kalv said.

Dael inclined his head. "I did it for no accolades. I owed it to Lyra."

"Who is this?" Everett asked, looking Dael up and down.

Lyra sucked in a breath through the pain. "Dael, my ex… kind of…"

"I was her betrothed," Dael finished for her. "We are no more, unless she comes to me willingly."

Everett nodded. "She won't be, so don't hold your breath."

"Why would you work for my father," Lyra asked her attacker. "What did he offer you that was so appealing you would try to kill me?"

"For my family here. I am Simea, last of my house," he answered. "He said he would give us land and wealth. My wife and children are human."

"Then why did you not come through the portal and petition the king?" Kalv demanded.

"How can we? The portals are closed to us," Simea spat. "The king has barred the way for those he deems unworthy."

Kalv frowned. "That is not true. After the Shen were defeated, all portals to Paladin were open. Who has told you such lies?"

"Let me guess—my father Hamon," Lyra said quietly. "I am sorry to tell you, he used you for his own gain. He wanted my death on your hands and my father had no intention of honoring any promise he made to you."

"It was all… lies?" Simea said incredulously and then horror crossed his face. "By the Gods, what have I done?"

"Nothing. I stopped you before you could ruin your life and that of your family," Dael said. "Shall I escort him back to Paladin so he can tell the king of Hamon's treachery?"

"I don't want him punished," Lyra spoke up. "He was as much a victim of my father's as I am. All he wanted to do was go home."

Simea's eyes filled with tears. "Princess, you have my utmost apologies, my life blood is now yours."

Lyra shook her head. "I don't want it, Simea. Just take your family home."

Kalv nodded to Dael. "Take him to his family, then take them to the king."

"Dael…" Lyra moved forward slowly and rested her head against his firm chest, and he put a large hand around her back. She spoke without looking up at him. "Thank you for saving me."

"I owe you that much, my princess… and so much more," Dael said gently.

She stepped back, and he nodded to them before escorting Simea away.

"So that's the ex, huh?" Everett said stiffly, and she could sense the jealousy rolling off him. "You seem… close."

"He just saved my life," Lyra said stiffly. "I really need to get home."

"The truck is trashed," Everett said.

"I'll take a ride share. Uncle Kalv, can you take care of this?" Lyra asked.

Kalv nodded. "It never happened."

Everett looked from him to her. "The call came in and I heard it over the police radio. How are you going to fix this?"

"It never happened," Kalv repeated. "Take my niece home, feed her, let her sleep and heal."

Everett gave a stiff nod. Lyra knew that he felt offended that Kalv, well, she and her people could make this whole situation disappear. He was accustomed to the sense of authority being a cop brought. Exposing Everett to her life meant he saw that humans may essentially be the low men on the totem pole. She would have to give him a bit more time before letting him know dragons weren't the only thing that roamed the nights. There were many a hunter across the world, even in Tucson. Humans were more prey than they realized.

In the car, he pulled her close, careful not to hurt her injured left side. Lyra let him. The sense of comfort made her pain less and she could feel the first hints that her second nature was free in her mind again and none too happy at being injured. At her home, he helped her from her clothes and his breath hissed through his lips at the dark purple bruises that marred her skin from her collar bone to her waist. Everett pressed soft kisses on her injuries before he pressed his forehead against hers. No words were needed, not right now.

Feeling semi human after her shower, she slipped a bathrobe over her naked body and downed seven over-the-counter pain medication pills. Everett had ordered her a meal from her favorite restaurant that delivered, even late at night. She ate and felt him silently assessing her as she devoured every bite. Her body would burn calories to knit her broken rib and fractured arm.

The muscles and tendons would weave back to normal, but she would consume many a meal to compensate for what her body was doing.

"Stay with me while I sleep," Lyra asked Everett in a moment of feminine weakness. She wasn't accustomed to asking, but on this night, she felt weak and wanted the safety of his arms.

He stood and held out a strong hand to her, silently, and together they walked to her bedroom. Everett got her settled under the thick piles of blankets before sliding between them on the opposite of the bed away from her injuries. Lacing her fingers with his and he turned to kiss her temple as the blurry edges of sleep took her under quickly. There would be more battles between them but not at that moment. Right now, Lyra and her dragon needed their mate. While Everett didn't understand her life, they had chosen him.

The official excuse on record was that she had the flu and had to take a week off. But in actuality, that was how long it took for her to heal after the car crash. If she was a full dragon in about forty-eight hours, she would have been back to normal, but her human half affected her ability to heal. She got updates from Everett when he came by every day. In fact, he only left to go to work and came right back to take care of her. Lyra had to admit being pampered wasn't bad at all.

Rita ended up turning witness against her father, and that got her some leverage for kidnapping and murder. Lyra didn't think it was fair that both she and Geoff got to live their lives while Monica was dead. But this was the FBIs brand of justice, the information outweighed a life. She tried to put it out of her head because she and Everett worked the case and brought the killer in for justice. It was all they could do, the deals made were above their pay grade. She would have to be happy that Bryce was home living with parents and probably wouldn't remember the terrors he faced at two years old.

Simea and his family were allowed to return to Paladin with King Orin's blessing. After hearing the treachery that Hamon conspired, including the attempt on her life, King Orin passed the judgement of him and he was banished from Paladin. They went to his house with the guardian to take him, to serve justice and the house was empty. His body was found on the rocks, the same area where Lyra's mother fell to her death. Lyra wondered if he chose death on his own terms or did madness finally drive him over the edge. She mourned his loss in a way. She was Princess Lyra, the last of the line of Hamon. The Queen of her house.

She would be going back to work the next day, with so much left unsaid between her and Everett. The argument they had while trying to find Bryce was never finished and while she accepted him as who he was it wasn't hard for her to have doubts about him. He seemed affectionate and caring and even bit his tongue when he came to her house to find Dael there with her Uncle to say goodbye.

"Going back home?" Everett asked.

Kalv nodded. "To get my family and head to Texas for the kids to finish school then home to Paladin for the summer solstice. Maybe we shall see you there."

"That would be interesting. Lyra said if the King says yes, she will show me your world," Everett answered.

"I think he will." Kalv shook his hand. "You've got a warrior's heart, Everett. Be good to my niece or… I have been known to partake in a human snack."

"Ha-ha, Lyra already told me you don't eat humans." Everett grinned. Kalv smiled in return. "Did she now?"

Dael nodded to Everett. "Human, goodbye."

"I can't say I'm sorry to see you go," Everett muttered.

Dael's eyes were devilish. "I have no doubt you'll see me again. After all,

my princess is here."

"She isn't yours," Everett called to his retreating back in irritation.

Dael said nothing, but she heard his laughter as he followed her uncle outside. She had no doubt that Deal still had an interest in her. Lyra could tell that Everett noted that as well and it grated on his nerves. Her mind focused on the present day and how she and her partner needed to talk. Things like this couldn't be swept under the rug. She'd seen what unspoken words could do to a relationship.

While she made dinner, she planned in her mind what to say to him. The portabella mushrooms were sautéing with the caramelizing onions. She made thick steaks in another of her copper frying pans. Salted, fingerling potatoes were in the oven baking to perfection to finish the meal. She would never be rail thin; her curves held two beings within it and both liked to eat. *I am a carnivore after all.* The thought filtered through Lyra's mind and caused her to smile. Forty-five minutes later, Everett walked into her house and called her name.

"Lyra, where are you… sauna?" Everett called out

She looked through the half wall that separated the kitchen from the wide expanse of the living room. "You can't smell the food? Do I cook in the sauna?"

He grinned and walked over. "After what we did in there, hell yeah you do."

Lyra shook her head. "You are incorrigible. Did you get the margarita mix I wanted?"

He held up the bag. "Two. I know how you and Trixie drink."

"My last day of impromptu vacation, I'm going out with a bang."

"I can help with that too." He came up behind her and kissed her neck. "The guys miss you. They keep asking when the human lie detector is coming back."

"They just want me to buy food," Lyra teased and cleared her throat. "Everett, we need to talk."

"Uh-oh, are you leaving me for Dael?" Everett asked.

She raised an eyebrow. "Been holding on to that one, huh?"

Everett took a beer from the fridge. "The dude has his eyes on you."

"His gaze is not his hand, so stop it. I am where I want to be," she said. "We are straying from the subject, the one we never finished after we took Bryce home."

"Lyra—"

"I need to speak first. There is always going to be an element of risk and lies to knowing who I am." Lyra opened the oven to check her potatoes as she worked. "I know that you need pure honesty in your life from those who are in it. I cannot assure you of that, but I can tell you that when it comes to us, I will never lie to you. But protecting myself and my second nature is imperative. Can you accept that?"

"I was an ass and I put my foot in my mouth." Everett placed his beer down and cupped her cheeks. "You are so unique, so beautiful, and have introduced me to a world only few know about. I was pissed that Trixie knew first and I acted like a douche. But never doubt that if it came down to protecting you with my life, I would."

"I would do the same for you," Lyra said huskily.

Everett kissed her, once then twice, and the third time the kiss deepened until they were both gasping for breath.

His voice was ragged when he pulled away. "Two questions, how long before Trixie gets here and how healed up are you?"

"We have an hour, and since it's Trixie about an hour and a half." Lyra whipped off her thin white t-shirt revealing no bra beneath. "The burners are off for now. Show me what you got, Officer Craig."

"In the kitchen?" Everett asked as she worked at the dark blue button-up shirt he wore.

"Scared of a few flames, Everett?" she teased. "A dragon's breath can melt glass."

"I would brave the fire just for you." He worked at her athletic leggings and brought them down over her bare feet.

She gasped when his lips touched the skin of her flat torso. "We have entirely too many clothes on."

"My thoughts exactly," he said against her skin.

When he came back up to stand close to her, Lyra pressed frantic kisses on his neck and then on the broad expanse of his chest. She watched as Everett closed his eyes in pleasure before he grabbed her and kissed her hungrily as he moved her backwards. Her body thumped against the fridge and the glass containers clanked together. Their tongues dueled and parried from one mouth to the next. It was her turn to back him against the wall. She licked and kissed down his body, and she felt his hand fist in the thick tresses of her hair.

Lyra had little to no inhibitions, but when it came to sex, it was like a whole new world was opened to her. Lyra tugged his pants down eagerly and took his boxers with them. As the barrier fell away, a low groan escaped Everett when she twined her tongue around the tip of his cock.

Lyra grasped his hard flesh in her hand and stroked firmly, and it matched the rhythm of her greedy mouth. She finally took his length deep into between her lips, inch by delicious slow torturous inch until his thighs flexed and he thrust himself deeper between her lips. While Lyra was innocent to lovemaking, she had quickly learned what he liked. Her tongue combined with the use of her hand made him groan her name in pleasurable agony. His harsh breathing filled her ears and with his hands buried in her hair, he fucked her mouth only fueling the pleasure between them.

"Okay stop, Jesus stop." Everett's voice was hoarse as he pleaded for a reprieve.

"You like how my mouth feels, yes?" Lyra gasped as he cupped her breast in his hand.

"Babe, if I tell you how hot your mouth makes me, I may explode before I bury myself inside you," Everett muttered.

A surprised laugh escaped her when he lifted

her like she weighed nothing, and the granite of her kitchen island was cool against her ass. His hands roamed all over her naked skin and down to her hips before he pushed her thighs apart. Lyra tilted her hips forward eagerly and watched as Everett got to his knees. She loved how his mouth felt on her sex, the ways he found and teased the tiny bud of pleasure hidden between its soft folds.

A cry escaped her when he flicked his tongue over the sensitive bud of her clit. Her hips jerked in response and soon the teasing seemed to leave him impatient because he wanted more. Lyra wanted him to take it all, everything, until she felt that release that left her weak in the knees. Everett grabbed her hips and pulled her more firmly against his mouth. She undulated her hips against the sensation of his mouth and tongue. With a primal grunt, he pulled her to him in one rough motion and continued to taste her, making low sounds of carnal lust.

"Oh, bless it, by the Gods, don't stop." Lyra's head tilted back as she moaned.

A groan was all that she heard, and Everett sucked on her clit and upped the ante by flicking his tongue in sweet repetition until she came on a shuddering cry. Lyra tugged at his shoulders, needing to feel his naked body against hers.

Everett returned her kisses with just as much need and desire, spearing his tongue deep into her mouth, and she wrapped her legs around his waist.

He was the fire in her blood, and her heart hammered their need through her veins. She immersed herself in every sensation each and every time they were together. Everett filled his palms with the heavy globes of her breasts, and she loved the feel of his hands against her skin. He took the upturned nipple into his mouth eagerly teasing one, then the other before sucking each of them in turn deep into his mouth. With each deep pull between his lips she felt it spear to her core.

"Do it again," Lyra pleaded and lifted her breast to him, offering more.

"I don't think I will ever stop wanting you," he whispered.

"It's all so good, I want to scream," she admitted. "What is it about you that turns me on so much?"

"Woman, that is the sexiest thing anyone has ever said to me," he said just before he kissed his way down her body again.

She shuddered in anticipation when his lips trailed down her smooth abdomen and back to where he found her soaking wet. He liked to watch her, and she met his gaze as sank his digit into her pussy. Lyra bit her lip as the walls of her sex clenched around his digit. She was trembling, it couldn't be helped. Lyra threw her head back in pleasure as he used his fingers to please her and his thumb to manipulate her clit. She whimpered when he blew against the sensitive bud. The flick of his tongue combined with the use of his hand drove her closer to the edge.

"Oh yes, yes…" Her voice rose with excitement. "I want you inside me so very badly."

It was like something in him snapped. He drove her to the edge of madness, with his lips, tongue, and fingers until Lyra screamed his name. Her orgasm made her toes point and her body jerk, yet Everett wasn't happy until he made her come again.

"I love how you come for me, without inhibition," Everett murmured. "It's so wild and free. I have never experienced anything like this before."

Everett was on his feet kissing her before she could answer. and she could taste her essence on his tongue. Lyra wrapped her leg around his waist, and she braced her hands on either side of the granite countertop. Her upturned nipples were there for his tasting and Everett pulled one into his mouth as he sank his cock deep within her at the same time.

Her cry was echoed by his low groan of pleasure against her flesh. The sensation, the feel of him gliding between the full lips of her pussy almost made her come again. She met his thrusts, lifting her hips each time to take more of him until their connection made a wet, slapping sound. Lyra looked at him, lips parted and saw his eyes piercing, filled with desire, watching every nuance she made.

"Do you want more?" He punctuated his words with deep thrusts. "Tell me you want to come."

"Give me more," Lyra demanded, her hips undulating against him eagerly. "Harder, I want to come, everything… I want it now."

"Ah shit…" Everett's voice was harsh, and he grabbed her hips while pounded into her.

He gave her everything she wanted and more. Everett watched her; she trembled under his gaze and it was as if he knew the exact moment she would find her release. He rubbed her clit with his thumb, and she tumbled off the edge of sanity into bliss. Lyra undulated her hips, and combined with the clenching of her sex, it seemed to take the last of his control. His body shuddered and tensed as his orgasm took hold. Everett grabbed her hips, taking hard and rough until she was crying out. The band of pleasure tightened once more.

Each thrust sent her higher and higher until Lyra felt like she was touching the stars. Reaching between them, she felt his balls tighten under her fingers, and Everett groaned her name when his seed filled her wet sex. Their kiss was hot, and she took his groans into her mouth just as she would his tongue. Together they slid to the floor, a mass of legs and arms all the while tasting each other's lips and flesh. Finally, she lay back against the hardwood floor and a deep contented sigh escaped her.

"Man, I like the way you cook," Everett chuckled.

"At some point, we should get up before Trixie finds us like this." Lyra kissed his bare chest. "Not that she'd mind."

"Seriously?" he asked intrigued. "Like a threesome thing?"

"No, you nut, like a dissertation of our sexual pleasure." She laughed. "She's getting her PhD in psychology."

"Ah well, I don't want to share you anyway," Everett said.

Lyra got to her feet and held out her hand. "Let's get a shower before our friend shows up and I can finish making our dinner."

"After we clean the counters of course." He took her hand and she levered him to his feet.

She nodded sagely. "Of course… Everett, there's more to my life I have to tell you, more to this world than you even know."

He pulled her in front of him as they walked toward the bathroom. "How about we cross that bridge when we come to it? Let's not overload my senses."

"Another time then," she said and laughed as he tickled her ribs.

This was only the beginning, there was much more to this world and if he was in her life as a partner on the force and the lover in her bed, he would have to know. But tonight, she would enjoy him and her best friend over good food and drinks. Tucson would need them to protect the city and at night she would teach him what lies in the darkness and the ways to survive it all. Tomorrow was another day.

The End

About the Author

Dahlia Rose is the USA Today best-selling author of contemporary, military romance with a hint of Caribbean spice. She was born and raised on a Caribbean island and now currently lives in Charlotte, North Carolina, with her five kids, who she affectionately nicknamed "The Children of the Corn," and her husband and longtime love who is also a honorable retired Army veteran. She has a love of erotica, dark fantasy, sci-fi, and the things that go bump in the night. With over six dozen books published Dahlia has become a reader favorite. Not only because of her writing but her vivacious attitude in talking to her fans online and at various events. Books and writing are her biggest passions, and she hopes to open your imagination to the unknown between the pages of her books.

Website: www.dahliaroseunscripted.com
Blog: www.dahliaroseunscripted.blogspot.com
Facebook: www.facebook.com/author.dahliarose
Twitter: www.twitter.com/dahliarose1029
Bookbub: https://www.bookbub.com/profile/dahlia-rose

www.ingramcontent.com/pod-product-compliance
Lightning Source LLC
Chambersburg PA
CBHW060542160726
47991CB00001B/419